P9-ELR-069

MILLENNIUM

"The Millennium Group, they really believe this stuff, then? Nostradamus and Revelations. . . ? The destruction of the world?"

Frank stared at him. A full minute passed before he replied. "They think we can't just sit back and wait for a happy ending."

Look for all the official books
based on the hit Fox television series

Millennium: The Frenchman
*Millennium: Gehenna**

*coming soon

MILLENNIUM

THE
FRENCHMAN

ELIZABETH HAND

BASED ON THE CHARACTERS
CREATED BY

CHRIS CARTER

HarperPrism
A Division of HarperCollinsPublishers

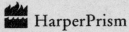

HarperPrism
A Division of HarperCollins*Publishers*
10 East 53rd Street, New York, N.Y. 10022-5299

ISBN 0-06-105800-9

HarperCollins®, ®, and HarperPrism® are trademarks of HarperCollins*Publishers*, Inc.

Cover illustration by Hamagami/Carroll & Associates

First printing: June 1997

Printed in the United States of America

Visit HarperPrism on the World Wide Web at
http://www.harpercollins.com

❖ 10 9 8 7 6 5 4 3 2 1

MILLENNIUM

THE
FRENCHMAN

MILLENNIUM
PROLOGUE

It comes like this: muted cries, the sound of panting, a crimson wave lapping at his feet. Unblinking eyes that will not turn away, the soft pressure of a mouth at his groin; the crimson waves crashing higher and higher still, until he can taste it in his mouth, bile and copper, blood streaming from the corners of his eyes, and the voice he hears is his own, the screams are his own though the blood, always, is not.

It comes like this, he comes like this: and afterward is left gasping on the shore, the tide receding, and nothing left but that taste in his mouth, and a trace of blood on his palms.

MILLENNIUM
CHAPTER

He stood just beyond the alley, shoulders hunched against an icy February rain that glazed the broken sidewalk, made a lurid scarlet beacon of the club's flickering neon sign.

THE RUBY TIP
SEATTLE'S HOTTEST!
LIVE GIRLS UNTIL 2:00 AM

For the hundredth time he read the words, mouth parted slightly so that his upper teeth bit into his lip. He grimaced, as though tasting something rank, then tugged his baseball cap down tight against the rain, crossed the alley, and shoved his way through the heavy steel door.

Industrial music pounded down the dark hallway, the jackhammer beat keeping time with the blood thrumming in his head. The reek of pine disinfectant warred with cigarette smoke and perfume, the fainter, spoiled scents of arousal and release. On either side of the corridor doors loomed, alternating red and green. Here and there the floor was flecked with peeling paint, cigarette butts, crumpled flyers: TIFFANEE BRIGHT: CALL ME 24 HRS!!! SUSHI CHIEF: WE DELIVER. A muffled *thunk* as one of the doors opened and closed. He looked up, saw a young woman with chic dark hair and heavy leather trench coat striding toward him, her high-heeled boots making a hollow sound on the linoleum. Other doors opened; men jostled soundlessly past each other, their glances, cold as rain, washing over the girl. She shook her hair back, mouth tight, and did not meet their predatory gaze. For a moment the man in the baseball cap stood there, watching her as she passed. Then he quickly turned and disappeared behind one of the green doors.

The woman continued on her way, hands thrust deep into her pockets. At the ticket desk she gave a perfunctory wave to the young man inside—Sammy, a good kid, didn't hassle the girls, did his best to weed out the weirdos when he could.

"I'm off," she announced.

Sammy slid another roll of quarters into the cash drawer, lifted his chin to acknowledge her. "Yup." He watched her sidle out the door, holding it open for a slight figure in rain-soaked jacket and tight jeans who hurried inside, her head tilted so as to avoid the eyes of the patrons milling around inside.

"Hey, Tuesday." Sammy smiled, self-consciously stroked the goatee he'd been working on for two weeks now. "How's it goin'?"

Tuesday shrugged. "What can I say? I'm here."

"Alrightee." Sammy swiveled in his chair to check out the next customer. "Later—"

Tuesday moved with practiced haste and hauteur down the corridor, elbowing past the men, who paused to stare at her, finally pushing open the door of the dancers' dressing room. A haze of smoke met her, and the throb of a Nine Inch Nails song from behind another door that led onstage. A pair of battered sofas were shoved against the walls beneath peeling music posters and a flyer from the Puget Sound Women's Health Care Center. Three dancers in work gear-leather bustier, candy pink baby-doll dress, black satin tap pants and bra-sprawled companionably on the couches, smoking and flipping through the latest rash of magazines brought in by Sammy. They looked up as Tuesday crossed to the clothes rack and began pulling out her night's costume.

"Hey, Tues."

"Your car running better?"

"There's some coffee, I just made it—"

Tuesday nodded, flashed a smile as she hung up her wet jacket and began peeling off a cable-knit sweater. "Thanks. Yeah, it was just an electrical glitch, the mechanic fixed it, only cost forty bucks. Thank God—"

Behind her the stage door flew open, and a willowy blonde in red bikini and matching push-up bra stalked in, her face damp, golden tendrils plastered across her forehead.

"Hey, Calamity," Tuesday greeted her. "How's it going?"

"Okay." Calamity looked over her shoulder as she hurried to the far wall, where a pay phone hung alongside a scrawled list of telephone numbers. "I want to make sure the baby-sitter hasn't left yet." She shoved a quarter into the slot, punched in her number, and leaned impatiently beside the phone, wincing as she pushed her long hair from her eyes. "Hey, Tuesday—that weird French guy's back."

Tuesday unhooked her plain white bra and pulled on a more provocative one, demi-cups and black lace edging her breasts. "The guy with the poetry?"

Calamity nodded. "Yeah. And—Oh, hi honey, it's Mommy! Is Cindy still there? Can I talk to her?"

Tuesday's face creased with sympathy as she watched the woman on the phone. She pulled off her jeans, pulled on a black G-string, then strode to where a cheap floor-length mirror listed on the wall by the stage door. The Nine Inch Nails song ended. The PA system roared into the opening chords of White Zombie's "More Human Than Human." Tuesday tugged her fingers through her thick hair, teasing it back from her face, then expertly ran cerise lipstick across her mouth, touched up the corners of her eyes with liner and mascara. She gave the mirror a parting moue, then turned and walked through the door and onto the dance floor.

The girls called it the Cage. An area roughly twenty by twenty feet square, blindingly lit by colored strobe lights that would, without warning, darken to violet or the sullen red of banked embers. Around its perimeter was a series of small square windows. Through these could be glimpsed shadowy figures, crouching or standing in their dark booths as they watched the girls onstage with dull, flattened eyes. Tuesday spun past the four other dancers, conscious of a faint flicker of attention as the furtive observers momentarily shifted their attention to her: The New Girl. She preened, half-closing her eyes and licking her lips seductively as she ran her fingers through her hair, whirling to give first one window, then the next, a view of her breasts straining from her push-up bra, the smooth hollow of her belly curving down to her pubis. Through the dully reflected sheen of black glass she caught the flicker of eyes here, a mouth there, as her hands dropped down, lingering upon the lacy edges of her bra. For a moment she shut her eyes, feigning ecstasy, then opened them.

In front of her was one of the observation windows. A figure stood behind it: the Frenchman. He was there two or three times a week, always wearing the same dark baseball cap and dark glasses, always bearing the same offering for the women inside the cage—a piece of paper scrawled with foreign words. French, Calamity said, though none of the girls ever got the chance to figure out what the messages actually said.

"Just as well," Brittany snorted once, when Calamity expressed curiosity about him. "Fucking weirdo, what else do you need to know?"

He was there now in front of Tuesday, holding up a handwritten piece of loose-leaf against the glass. Tuesday smiled at him, a smile that was close to a sneer; then shimmied right up to his window, taunting him. Fingers tracing the front of her G-string, then moving slowly up between her thighs, across her taut abdomen to where her breasts threatened to spill from her bra. She toyed with the snap there, starting to open it, head thrown back, eyes closed for just an instant—

But when she opened them again, he was gone.

Backstage in the dressing room, Brittany put the finishing touches to her makeup, then flounced out into the Cage. Behind her Calamity buttoned her flannel shirt, shrugged into a shapeless wool sweater, and pulled on her Doc Martens. She glanced at her watch—ten past one—and swore under her breath. She'd promised the sitter she'd be back by twelve-thirty.

"Gotta fly," she called out to the other girls, sweeping up her backpack and parka. "See ya—"

Just then Sammy poked his head through the door. "Hey," he said, cocking a thumb at Calamity. "You've got a private."

Calamity shook her head. "I'm off," she said, zipping her parka. "Sorry."

"Two hundred bucks for ten minutes."

The girls on the couch turned to stare first at Sammy, then Calamity. "Well, shit," Calamity said after a moment. "I better call the sitter . . ."

And she began to get undressed.

The private booth is a heated darkness. Smells of copper, of musk, of sweat and damp tobacco and semen. Of sex. Inches from his face the small square window fogs as his breath blooms upon it. On the other side of the glass writhes a woman. Pale blond hair cascades to her shoulders, is swept back up again as her fingers stroke the heavy tendrils and she croons in counterpoint to the languorous music seeping into the booth from a hidden sound system.

"Do you like to watch me?" The woman drops her hands, snakes them suggestively across her breasts. *"I know you like to watch me . . ."*

He says nothing.

"*Tell me what you want,*" the woman whispers. She purses her mouth in a little-girl pout, half closes her eyes as she sidles up to the window and licks her lips. "*Tell me. . . ?*"

In the booth he takes a step backward. His heart is thudding in his chest as he nods, quickly, then begins to mumble, "I want to see you dance . . . I want to see you dance on the blood-dimmed tide."

"*You like to watch me, don't you?*"

He exhales, and her body blooms, an explosion of black and crimson, caustic flowers opening up as her eyes recede into black pits and her lips peel back from her gums to reveal naked bone, blood oozing from raw stumps where her teeth had been. He pants, sweat trickling into the corners of his mouth. Behind the woman a faint glister of red forms on the surface of the walls, as she cups her breasts and leans forward. Corruption falls away from her: she is young and desirable once more, her mouth a crimson slash, her creamy thighs opening to him though he no longer sees her; his eyes are riveted by the wall behind her. Where the dull gleam of scarlet has become a ribbon, a rivulet, blood pearling and then pooling down to the floor, where it runs in an ever-widening stream to lap at the woman's high heels.

"You like to watch my body," she breathes, twirling on one foot so that blood sprays her bare ankle. *"I know you like it . . ."*

His breath comes faster and faster still, his hand begins to shake. He pushes himself closer to the window, and his voice trembles as he whispers, the words lost in the darkness.

In front of him she is moving faster as well, keeping time with his breathing. She caresses her neck, her shoulder blades, her stomach. Streaks of blood trail from her fingertips as they map her body, moving from beneath her navel to the tops of her thighs. The walls seem to breathe, to shudder, blood coursing down them until the room is filled with blood, there is blood everywhere . . .

". . . I know you like it. Don't be shy."

. . . everywhere, his hands are damp with it, her hair flings off red droplets as she arches her back and shakes her head, eyes shut tight as he groans, his mouth struggling to speak—

". . . this is the second death . . ."

And still the blood comes, a sanguine waterfall that splashes up around her thighs as she dances, and he watches her, his voice louder now as he clutches at the window in front of him.

"... abominable ..." he mumbles, though she hears nothing. She looks at him, and his mouth does not move.

"*I know you like it,*" she repeats, eyelashes sweeping down to hide her gaze as she dips her head, then glances up at him through a fringe of smoke and flame. "*I know you like it . . .*"

He groans and blinks, eyes tearing.

From the walls flames erupt, roaring down and into the room as though blood were tinder, fuel-soaked paper, hair held above a candle. The lake of blood shimmers, then bursts into a blaze of gold and black and scarlet, blinding. The flames writhe and dance, encircling the woman, who moves heedlessly through the fire, even as her skin crackles and curls away, drops of fat spattering against the window glass as her mouth moves brokenly, and he watches her hair turn to ash, her fingers splayed into twigs that sputter and twist into smoke. His own voice roars into nothingness as he gasps and falls backward against a chair, the woman's last words echoing in his ears as flames engulf the room. The stench of blood fills his nostrils as a single tear falls upon his cheek.

"*I know you like it.*"

MILLENNIUM
CHAPTER

3

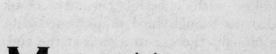

Morning struck the city, sun instead of its customary fog and rain. On a hillside facing east, Frank Black navigated his family's red Cherokee, blinking as light streamed through the dashboard and across his lean face.

"I think someone's trying to peek," he announced, smiling as he glanced at his wife in the seat beside him. In her lap their six-year-old daughter, Jordan, gasped and clapped her own hands over her mother's, already tightly pressed against her eyes.

"No peeking, Mommy!"

Catherine smiled and shook her head, not moving her fingers from her eyes. "Okay. You tell me when, Jordan."

Frank's smile broadened. He eased the car around a curve, passing beneath apple trees that would be full-leafed and flowering come spring, and then onto a broad side street, where neat bungalows and carpenter Gothic cottages were scattered like children's toys amid well-kept lawns, box-tree hedges, a garden where expired sunflowers still leaned over a trellis. On the sidewalk a boy cycled past, turning to stare at the Cherokee with cheerful curiosity. Frank nodded, as though he'd orchestrated this, then brought the car to a stop at the curb halfway down the block, behind a moving van. He turned to Jordan, peering up at him from beneath tousled dark curls like her mother's. For a long moment he gave in to the indulgence of looking at them both. He fought the customary surge of anxiety that had dogged him on the long cross-country drive from D.C., fought the stab of fear and horror like the memory of a bad dream, a dream he had finally managed to forget: that was all behind him now, this was a new home, a new life . . .

"Daddy?" Jordan's voice broke his reverie.

Frank blinked, looked up to see her squirming impatiently on Catherine's lap. "Now?"

Frank laughed and nodded: *Now*.

"Okay, Mommy!" Jordan cried, leaning over to bang on the window. "You can look now!"

Catherine composed her face into a semblance of dignity, took her hands from her eyes, and gazed out the window. For a moment Frank watched her anxiously. Then, "Oh Frank!" she exclaimed, elated. "You had it painted—"

And as she clambered excitedly from the car, Jordan spilling onto the sidewalk after her, he knew that, at last, everything was going to be all right.

"Is this our new house, Daddy?" cried Jordan. "Is this it?"

Frank climbed from the car and joined them at the edge of green lawn, nodding. "Our new yellow house," he said.

Above the slope of close-trimmed grass and clover gleamed a sunny yellow Craftsman-style bungalow, the trim around its windows and dormers glowing white. Leaded glass in the second-story windows sparked prismlike in the morning sun. On the porch several fuchsias hung in wicker baskets, a gift from the realtor. Catherine gazed at it transported, then began to walk dreamily up the sidewalk. Behind her, Jordan's hand slipped into her father's as they followed her.

Inside, the movers had already set the heavier furniture in vaguely homey configurations: sofa, overstuffed armchairs, Jordan's rocking chair in the living room; wicker end tables and reading lamps in the sunroom; and boxes and boxes everywhere else.

Christ! Frank shook his head, wondering what on earth they could all be filled with— books? dishes? Jordan's collection of Legos? A few feet away an old Victorian coat stand leaned forlornly against the wall, beside the mirror from Jordan's dresser. He caught a glimpse of himself, trapped within the bright pink-and-yellow frame: a tall, lean man, his dark hair stitched with gray, eyes deep-set and serious, though not humorless; deep channels etched around his eyes and mouth. It was not a face that smiled easily, but it was a face that compelled trust. A crony of Frank's at the bureau had once quipped that Frank could be a stand-in for the angel Gabriel: "A mug like that is only good for breaking bad news from the Big Guy." The remark hadn't stung, because they all knew the truth behind it. Most of Frank's job had involved being on the receiving end of very bad news indeed.

"Oh, Daddy, *there* they are!"

His daughter ran past him, squealing with delight as she recognized a carton with her name on it, and began pulling out stuffed animals. Frank grinned wryly, then edged aside as the moving men came through again, this time carrying the kitchen table. The sight of them working galvanized him: he hefted a carton into his arms and was just turning to follow them into the kitchen when Catherine's voice rang out.

"Frank? Can you come here?" At her serious tone his heart began to beat too fast. He looked up to see her on the second-floor landing, her face drawn. "There's something here."

He practically flung the carton from him, his feet echoing loudly on the stairs. "Catherine?" he called when he hit the landing, trying to keep his voice calm. There was no answer. "Catherine?"

He started down the hall, his face grim. It was only when he reached the bedroom, and saw Catherine standing just inside the door with a rapturous expression, that his fear stilled.

"What is it?" he asked softly.

She said nothing, only put her arms around his neck and drew him to her. She kissed him deeply, her warmth and the curve of her hands about him as familiar as his own heartbeat. For a moment they lingered there, leaning against the doorframe. Then Frank drew back, just enough that he could stare down into her green eyes and see there what he was looking for.

"I'm so happy right now," she whispered. For an instant tears brightened her gaze. "I think this move was the right thing. I really do, Frank."

He nodded, feeling anxiety peel away from him like old paint. "I do, too. It feels like home."

From outside came a faint thump, a familiar whirring sound. They both turned to stare out the window, to where the same boy Frank had seen earlier was whooshing past on his bike, another folded newspaper already in his hand to hit the next front stoop. They watched until he was out of sight, then began to laugh: it was too perfect.

He grinned and shook his head. "Pinch me."

She did, grabbing his ass playfully and pulling him back to her. They kissed again, sunlight striking Frank's eyelids as he whispered, "Home. It feels like home."

MILLENNIUM
CHAPTER

4

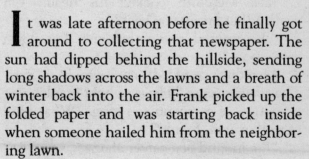

It was late afternoon before he finally got around to collecting that newspaper. The sun had dipped behind the hillside, sending long shadows across the lawns and a breath of winter back into the air. Frank picked up the folded paper and was starting back inside when someone hailed him from the neighboring lawn.

"Hello there!"

He turned and saw a balding man in his late fifties waving his own newspaper. Pleasant-faced, with round amiable features and a bright red cardigan buttoned a little too tightly across an ample stomach. "Hi, Jack Meredith," the man went on, crossing the lawn and beaming. "I guess we're going to be neighbors."

"Frank Black."

The other man took Frank's hand and pumped it welcomingly, then tucked his paper beneath his arm and rocked back on his heels. "So! Frank. Where you folks from?"

A twinge of unease flickered through Frank, but he pushed it down. "We've been in Washington, D.C., for ten years," he said firmly. "But originally my wife and I are from here in Seattle."

Jack Meredith cocked his head. "Oh yeah? What brings you back?"

"We wanted to come home. Put down some roots."

Meredith nodded approvingly. "Sure. That makes sense." His gaze held Frank's, just a fraction of a second too long. "What kind of work you in, Frank?"

"I'm in kind of a career change."

Meredith's eyebrows shot up. "Oh. Got anything lined up?"

Frank gave him a measuring look, then smiled. "I'm doing some consulting."

"Oh yeah?" Meredith looked pleased.

"Well, can we invite you folks over for dinner this week?" With a grin, he glanced over his shoulder at the bright yellow porch, where a Big Wheels bike and Little Tikes playhouse had already taken up residence. "We see you have a little girl."

"Thank you. I'll tell my wife."

"You do that," said Meredith. As Frank walked back to the porch, his neighbor's voice boomed cheerfully behind him. "Hey, Frank—you couldn't have picked a nicer place to come back to."

Frank smiled again, then turned his attention to the newspaper in his hand. He slipped off the rubber band, unfolded the paper, and let his eyes rove across it until he found the headline.

And stopped.

He read the headline, splashed across the top of the page in one-inch type.

MOTHER FOUND MURDERED IN HOME
5-Year-Old Daughter Hid From Slayer

Beneath the subheading, the sweet-faced image of a young woman with long blond hair smiled up at him.

"Frank?" On the porch the screen door creaked open. Catherine stepped out, head tilted curiously as she gazed down at her husband. "Frank? Who was that you were—"

The words died as he raised his face to the last faint rays of sunlight. His expression taut, eyes kindling as he looked past her, all but unseeing, and thought, *It never ends, it never ends: it never, ever ends.*

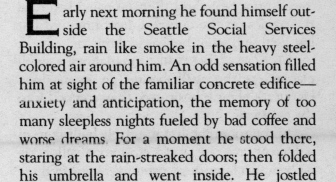

Early next morning he found himself outside the Seattle Social Services Building, rain like smoke in the heavy steel-colored air around him. An odd sensation filled him at sight of the familiar concrete edifice—anxiety and anticipation, the memory of too many sleepless nights fueled by bad coffee and worse dreams. For a moment he stood there, staring at the rain-streaked doors; then folded his umbrella and went inside. He jostled through the crowd of people hurrying to work, social workers and uniformed officers, eager-looking attorneys in power suits, administrative

aides still yawning as they moved aside to let
Frank into the elevator. There was the same
stale smell of recycled air, of laser ink and
steam tables in the employee cafeteria below.
The same everyday look of people going to
work; the same everyday marvel of men and
women meeting crises and horror and heart-
break with professional calm.

The third floor was as it had always been.
Seemingly endless ranks of cubicles, each
with its glowing computer screen; men and
women whose urgent expressions unexpect-
edly gave way to ironic laughter; the occasional crackle of a uniformed officer's
walkie-talkie. Frank strode past them all,
ignoring the openly curious looks that followed him. Now and then he paused to read
the names on the cubicles, frowning, until at
last he found what he was looking for.

LT. ROBERT BLETCHER, proclaimed a small
plaque on the wall beside an open door.
HOMICIDE. Frank hesitated, then stepped into
the doorway.

In the room a tall, formidably built man in
a discreet gray suit and testosterone yellow tie
sat behind a large desk, listening as one of three
detectives read from a computer printout.

"Nothing on that one-six that came
through," the detective said. He glanced at

another printout on the conference table in front of him. "And the rest'll take a few hours to process . . ."

Lieutenant Bletcher nodded. "Tell 'em a couple of hours is all they're gonna get," he replied, fingering a pencil. "And call that guy over in—"

Bletcher suddenly fell silent. His eyes fixed on the gaunt figure in the doorway. "I think I've just seen a ghost," he said, and got to his feet.

A thin smile touched Frank's mouth. "Hey, Bletch."

The detectives swiveled as the burly lieutenant crossed the room, grabbing Frank's hand and shaking it so happily that Frank had to move quickly to keep from being thrown off-balance. "Jesus! What are you doing here, Frank?"

Frank shrugged, letting Bletcher guide him into the room. "We moved back to Seattle."

Bletcher nodded. "You and Catherine?"

"Yeah. We missed the weather."

Bletcher turned to the other men, clapping a hand on Frank's shoulder. "Hey, this is Frank Black. He used to work homicide here. Before he became a big star at the FBI. Frank: Bob Giebelhouse, Pete Norton, Roger Kamm."

A subdued chorus of greetings. Then one

of the men—Giebelhouse—leaned across the conference table, eyes narrowing as he stared more closely at Frank. "Hey—you're the guy who caught the guy—that serial killer who ate his victims. Whatsisname—"

Frank nodded once, his face a mask. "Leon Cole Piggett."

Giebelhouse snapped his fingers. "Yeah! Hey, I was always curious. How did he prepare them?"

The lines around Frank's mouth grew more tight. "In a skillet," he said, his expression unreadable. "With potatoes and onions."

Giebelhouse snorted with disgusted laughter. "Jesus Christ!" he said, turning to share his amusement with the other detectives. "Can you believe that?"

Frank gave the three a cool look. Then he raised his eyes to Bletcher. "You got a minute?" he asked in a low voice.

Bletcher tipped his head. "Yeah. Sure—"

They stepped out of the office and walked down the hall. "How's work?" asked Frank.

"Homicide rate's a record low." Bletcher grinned, a little smugly. "Thirty-four this year."

"Congratulations."

Bletcher chuckled, lifting his hand as they passed several other people. "I'd like to take all the credit, but the truth is we've got some damn fine paramedics."

Frank permitted himself an ironic smile. They reached the end of the corridor and started down another, this one less crowded with cubicles and foot traffic. Frank glanced around, then asked softly, "What about this woman two days ago? The one with the little girl?"

Bletcher's face darkened. "She was a stripper," he said curtly. "Worked a peep show. Somebody obviously wanted more than a peep."

Frank stared at him appraisingly. "You're keeping the details from the press," he said at last.

Bletcher sighed. "It was bloody," he said, and shot Frank a grim, sunken look. "And cruel."

Frank said nothing; only nodded. After a moment he asked, "How's the little girl?"

"She's in custody down at DSHS."

"Did she witness the murder?"

Bletcher stopped in front of a fire door. "No, she didn't." He fixed the other man with a hard, wondering stare. "You here looking for work, Frank?"

Frank's cold eyes reflected the EXIT sign's ruby glare. "Sexual homicide. That's what I did for ten years, Bletch."

"And I hear it pushed you into early retirement."

The lieutenant's edgy tone softened. He gazed at Frank expectantly, but his friend said nothing; only stood there, his gaunt face dipped in shadow. A minute passed, then Frank said, "Any chance you could take me down to see the body?"

Bletcher continued to stare at him. Finally he nodded, once. "Come on."

In his years with the bureau, Frank had heard various morgues described as charnel houses, slaughterhouses, laboratories, even cathedrals: spaces desecrated or sanctified by death, yet retaining still the sense of a place set apart from the profane world, populated by physicians and coroners and medical researchers and, yes, corpses.

But to Frank, a morgue was a factory: simple as that. The dead were brought in, their flesh still warm sometimes, their faces still tight with the tales of their dying, bodies clothed and clothing torn, or worn, or bloodied: but each corpse a book to be opened, a mystery to be solved within spirals of DNA and loops of arteries, viscera and teeth and fingernails. The dead entered the morgue clothed in their traumas; protected, even, by their secrets. But when they left they all looked the

same, tagged and cleansed, bagged like so
many overprocessed bits of gristle and bone.

Factories, Frank thought grimly as he followed Bletcher downstairs.

This one was no different. A vast room,
warehouse-sized, illuminated by banks of fluores-
cent tubes hanging in rows high overhead, so
high that the light when it reached the floor was
scant, faintly greenish, like a sheen of ice on the
slick tile. Metal tables rose like islands in an arc-
tic sea, with here and there a technician or
orderly leaning over a pale form, and gurneys
scattered between them like waiting ships.
There was the barely detectable scent of spoiled
meat, the lactose smell of refrigerant, and an
underlying chemical sweetness, embalming fluid
and alcohol and disinfectant. It was cold enough
that Frank's breath fogged the air, and he shuddered, shrugging deeper into his suede jacket.

"This way." Bletcher inclined his head to
where a pathologist in white jacket and steel-
rimmed glasses sat perusing a folder of
autopsy records. "I called down already,
they're expecting us—"

The pathologist looked up, nodding as he
got to his feet. "Curt Massey," he said.

Frank's gaze flicked over him. "Frank
Black. We're here about the stripper."

Massey took in Frank's weathered face,

the unsettling intensity of his pale eyes. After a moment he stared back down at the papers in his hand. "She went down fighting. I can tell you that."

Frank tipped his head almost imperceptibly, as though listening to far-off music. The pathologist went on, "Blunt trauma and antemortem impact abrasions on her upper torso. She was a strong woman. Took some work to subdue her."

From behind them came the whimper of rubber wheels against the polished floor, the creak of metal. Frank and Bletcher turned in unison, to see an assistant pathologist pushing a stainless-steel gurney through a set of double doors at the room's far end. Between the gurney's railings a black body bag glistened.

"But then the killer was no weakling, either," the pathologist was saying. He beckoned the aide to bring the gurney alongside the table. As he did so Frank felt a small jolt at the base of his skull, a familiar burst of heat that extended into his eyes, so that for a moment he was blinded. He blinked, swallowing as he quickly shook his head, trying to focus before the vision was gone.

But it was too fast to capture. Instead he found himself sucked into the gaze of the assistant pathologist, a moon-faced youngish man, maybe in his late twenties, with pock-marked spongy skin that looked as though it would dent if you pressed a finger against it. For just an instant his gaze held Frank's: a muddy gaze, eyes too easily stirred by fear or anxiety into a stealthy, blank reflection of whatever they saw. Then he turned away, handing a clipboard to Massey and waiting while he initialed it. Massey returned the clipboard. The aide left.

"All right—" The pathologist pulled the gurney closer to where Bletcher and Frank waited. When he reached to unzip the body bag Frank stopped him, touching Massey's wrist lightly but commandingly as he looked into Bletcher's face.

Screams . . .

Bletcher frowned. "Frank?"

Screams.

A child's wailing voice, thin with terror. And another voice, torn between shrieks and gasping, a noise like canvas being shredded with a knife. Counterpoint to these a dull keening, mindless, deeper than the other sounds: a man. From the base of Frank's neck heat radiates in a web of flame, racing beneath his skin to blaze beneath his eyes. Which stare unblinking at a lamp thrown across a carpeted floor, magazines flying helter-skelter. The arm of a teddy bear poking from beneath a couch. An arm splayed limply across the carpet. Sanguine warmth that patters across his cheeks, the corners of his eyes, a crimson web stretching across his entire face.

"He severed her head."

The words fell from him, cold stone. Bletcher stared disbelieving into Frank's distant eyes. Beside him the pathologist waited a beat, then nodded.

"No mean task, let me tell you," he said with a grimace.

Frank licked his lips, tasting salt and copper. He fought nausea, the sense that he was being shoved into an airless room. "What was the position of her body when they found her?"

Massey's reply was cool, uninflected; but his eyes showed a spark of something like fear. "She was on her back with her arms crossed over her chest."

Frank's gaze narrowed. His posture grew rigid, as though he were a hunting dog on point, and he stared with almost manic intensity at the body bag in front of him.

About him the room shimmers into another room, walls dappled with crimson, black-and-crimson shadows dancing against incandescent white. There is an instant of near silence. The screams still as though they are a rain that stopped. Only instead of wind, or sunlight, there is an awful panting, and from somewhere far away frenzied scuffling, a small animal frantically trying to escape. A metallic stench fills his nostrils, and the smell of burning, a bare bulb singeing cheap carpet. Between his fingers is the bite of something cold and slicked with moisture. At his feet a sleeping woman lies on her back.

Frank blinked: sleeping, no. He said, "You didn't find a murder weapon, but it was something he took from the crime scene."

Bletcher watched him, fascinated and repelled, and nodded.

"She was clothed," Frank went on, speaking as though in a dream. "There was no evidence of any sexual assault."

The pathologist stared at Frank in amazement. After a moment he turned to Bletcher, confused.

But Bletcher wouldn't meet his look: his gaze remained on Frank, impelled to watch though he wanted to tear away, he wanted to see anything but this man with the dark in his eyes.

"What else?" demanded Bletcher.

She lies on the carpet, arms folded as in prayer, blond hair a pool about her face. Her hands look gloved in red, and there are red petals strewn across her cheeks and brow. The odor of scorched polyester fades into the stink of blood and excrement.

Frank's voice twisted, as though the words sought to burrow back inside him. "He cut off her fingers."

The pathologist sucked his breath in, his bemusement curdling into repugnance. "The man with the x-ray eyes."

Next to him Frank continued to stare fixedly, obsessively at the closed body bag. A muscle at the corner of his mouth twitched, a seam of ice giving way to floodwaters. "What did hair and fiber turn up?" he asked.

Bletcher bared his teeth. His expression mirrored the pathologist's detached revulsion. "Maybe you should tell me." When Frank refused to rise to this, he said, "Two head hairs from a black male."

Frank closed his eyes for an instant, opened them again. It seemed he might speak, and Bletcher waited expectantly. Instead Frank spun on his heel and walked away. His soft tread echoed through the cavernous space, the steel fire door slammed behind him as he entered the stairwell and started back to the upper level.

The pathologist watched him go, shaking his head. "How's he do that?"

Bletcher stared after Frank's solitary figure, wincing slightly as the fire door banged shut. "I don't know," he said at last. "Lucky guesser." With no further farewell, he hurried across the room.

Once in the stairwell Bletcher took the steps two at a time, huffing a little at the exertion. "Frank!" he called. "Frank—"

At the top of the stairs Frank waited, face set into a preternaturally calm mask. Bletcher came up beside him, panting. "You obviously didn't come down just to say 'hi', Frank. What are you doing here?"

Frank hesitated. Then, "I've seen this M.O. before," he said. A flicker of annoyance crossed Bletcher's face, but Frank's voice remained utterly composed, and convinced. "I know the patterns and the profile."

The lieutenant shifted his weight, barely keeping his impatience in check. "So what's the profile?"

"He'll kill again."

Bletcher took a deep breath. "Look. She was a working girl," he said, finally giving vent to his frustration. "A target."

Frank shook his head. "That's not why he chose her."

"Why did he choose her?"

"I don't know yet." Bletcher's mouth grew

tight. Before he could interrupt, Frank nodded very slightly and gave him a conciliatory glance. "Listen, Bletch. I'm working with a consulting group. These guys have a lot of experience with this sort of thing. They could have a look."

The stocky man bridled. "My guys are good, Frank."

"I know."

"I've got three detectives assigned to this," Bletcher continued heatedly, his voice rising. "What do I tell them?"

Frank's gaze grew hard. "That the killer's going to be hard to catch. They could use some luck—"

He pushed open the door leading out. "—Or some help."

With a grudging nod the lieutenant watched him go. Frank's shoulders hunched as he made his way through the crowded lobby. When the other man's spare form had been swallowed by the mob, Bletcher sighed. The door closed softly as he turned and trudged the rest of the way up to his office.

MILLENNIUM

CHAPTER

He went to The Ruby Tip. An alley where the sun never hit the pavement, where Frank could almost be grateful for the rank odors of rotting food and mildew: God only knew what you might smell otherwise. He'd never been there before, but he knew where he was. One of those places where everything got put on hold—reality, trust, fidelity, even faith. *I'm only doing it for the money. I'm only doing it for a little while. I'm only doing it till the kids are out of the house. I'm only doing it because I have to.*

But nothing stops them from doing it, Frank

thought somberly, standing outside for several
minutes in the sleety rain and watching as
men passed each other silently on the club's
front step. *Nothing stops the girls from dancing,
and nothing stops these guys from coming, not
even a murder.* He clenched his jaw, feeling
the familiar pressure beginning behind his
eyes, at the base of his neck, then tugged his
jacket tight around his shoulders and went
inside.

Pulsing music filled the corridor. Frank
winced, shoving past a man mopping the
floor inside a private booth. Industrial green
and rust red doors lined the hallway, bad
teeth waiting to be pulled from a diseased
mouth. He slowed to look at the Polaroids
taped to the private booths, overexposed
images of women defined by big hair and big
breasts, names like syrupy drinks: Tiffannee,
Brandy, Amber Lee. When he reached the
door that read TUESDAY he stopped. He gazed
at the picture there, wondered fleetingly why
the killer had chosen Calamity and not this
girl. Both shared the same sweet bland looks,
the same suicide blond hair, the same can-
tilevered cleavage in a cheap Victoria's Secret
knockoff. His eyes narrowed, but there was
no rush of warmth across his spine, no spate
of infernal images that might provide an

answer. He took a deep breath and went inside.

It was a claustrophobic space, dimly lit by a single red bulb hanging overhead. Breathy, piped-in music made the cubicle seem even smaller, all *oooohs* and moans and eerie, synthesized female voices. There was a metal folding chair, a large crumpled box of tissues on the floor beside it. The smell of pine disinfectant was so strong it made his eyes water. Frank moved the chair aside, standing in front of the window that filled the wall before him. The other side of the glass was covered by a tatty red velvet curtain. There was a slot in the wall beside the window. Frank withdrew his wallet, took out several bills and creased them so they'd fit into the slot, then stuffed them inside.

He waited. After a moment, a hand appeared inside the window and pulled the curtain aside, revealing the young woman in the Polaroid. Prettier than she'd looked in the photo, but more vulnerable, and tired: heavy foundation makeup, black mascara flecking her cheeks, lips chapped beneath pink gloss. She wore a red satin bikini bottom and matching push-up bra. As the curtain disappeared her gaze met Frank's for an instant, flicked away as her mouth curled into a pouting smile.

"Hi. You caught me." She arched her back so that her hair flowed down her shoulders, traced the outlines of her breasts with both hands. She had a sweet, deliberately childish voice and guileless sky-blue eyes. "I was just thinking of something nasty."

Frank shook his head. "I just want to talk."

Tuesday writhed in time to the music, mouth parting as she mimicked the echoing moans that filled the room. "Talk to me," she murmured. "Tell me what you want."

Frank reached inside his jacket and pulled out the newspaper photo of Calamity. Without a word he held it up to the window. For a moment Tuesday continued to sway and grind; then she saw the picture. Abruptly she stopped. She straightened and crossed her arms protectively across her breasts as she glared at Frank.

"You knew her, didn't you?" he asked.

At first he thought it would be a waste of time, that she wouldn't answer. The guileless blue eyes suddenly went cold, almost hateful; Frank imagined if he looked close enough to see tinted contact lenses, her eyes wouldn't really be blue, either. Finally she spit, "This isn't an interrogation booth."

"I'm not a cop."

She licked her lips, no longer seductively but nervously. "Well, I've already given my statement."

Frank tried to catch her gaze. She seemed determined not to look him in the eye. "I might be able to figure out who killed her," he said.

"Yeah?" This time her eyes did lock with his. A faint pleading note crept into her challenging tone. "How?"

Frank dipped his head slightly. "Tell me about her?" he asked.

Tuesday hugged her arms tighter around herself. She looked across the tiny interior of her booth, as though she might read something there, or find someone else to answer for her. Finally she began to speak.

"Her name was Calamity. She didn't hook, she didn't do drugs, she didn't even smoke. She danced for the money, so she could raise her little girl. There's not much else to know," she ended sadly.

"Did she have any fans? Any freaks?"

Tuesday's eyes glittered. "If you didn't notice, the clientele here isn't exactly the picture of moral rectitude," she said dryly. "They'd applaud, but it takes both hands."

Frank gave her a half smile: *touché*. For

another instant Tuesday looked right back at him, and he could see everything in her tired eyes: the suburbs and father she'd fled for Seattle, the video jobs that didn't pan out, the one-bedroom apartment she had to share with two other girls so she'd have enough money left over for community college. Another moment, and he felt he might divine her real name.

"Did you see anyone here the night she was murdered?" he asked gently. "Anyone who might have followed her home?"

"I stopped looking at their faces a long time ago."

He fought to keep the urgency from his voice. "Can you think of any reason someone might have killed her?"

"A reason?" Tuesday stared at him as in disbelief, then quickly looked away. "Men don't need *reasons*." Her voice trembled between rage and fear, and he saw her blink back tears. "All they need is an excuse."

Pity welled in him. He stared at the floor, no longer wanting to subject this woman to his gaze, then glanced up at her one last time before preparing to leave.

She is on fire. Flames curling around her breasts, her bra charred to black ash, hair candling like molten wire. Her mouth gapes open but no sound comes forth, only a stream of blood like spittle, roiling into steam and smoke as she thrashes within the inferno. Blood splashes against her thighs and waist, rains across her shoulders and splatters her face.

As he watched her Frank gasped, involuntarily started toward her.

Then it was gone: no flames, no blood, nothing but a weary young woman with chipped nail polish and sweat staining the edges of her brassiere. Frank stared at her. After a moment he nodded, pulled an extra bill from his wallet, and stuffed it into the money slot.

"I'm sorry. Thanks for your time." He was heading for the door when Tuesday's voice stopped him.

"There's a guy." Her tone was resigned, but her eyes held a hint of reluctant gratitude. "He holds up poetry to the window."

"What does it say?"

She shook her head. "I don't know. It's in French. We call him the Frenchman."

"Has he ever solicited anyone?"

"No, but he paid her for a private."

Frank nodded, trying to keep his voice even. "They have a camera in here?"

She hesitated. Surveillance cameras were

illegal, of course, but he knew plenty of places had them. Before he could say anything else, Tuesday stepped backward. She tilted her head back, and her eyes flickered almost imperceptibly, indicating a spot above Frank's head.

"Don't tell them I told you," she said in a low voice.

He looked up, to the far back corner of the private booth. A telltale laser red point of light glowed there.

Bingo, thought Frank. He glanced at Tuesday, allowed himself a quick smile of thanks. She gazed back at him, her expression unreadable. A moment later the heavy velvet curtain was drawn back across the window, and he was alone once more.

Night falls; but then it is always night, for him it is always dark. Rain slides across the windshield and there is a distant rough murmur, as of waves or thunder. He drives across the bridge, against the flow of traffic heading toward the city behind him. He can see it in the rearview mirror, a glister of green and red and yellow and white against the darkness, skyline like a fallen Christmas tree, lights unraveled and scattered about Puget Sound. People complain about the lights, saying they ruin the sky, make it impossible to see the stars—as if it had ever been possible to see the stars in this city, with its endless rain—saying that they ignite the night and drive the darkness away.

But the man Tuesday called the Frenchman knows this is pure madness. He knows there are not enough lights on earth to drive this dark away. Not now.

Not tonight.

Ahead of him an exit ramp leads down to a little-used street that parallels the wilder precincts of Volunteer Park. He turns off, drives for several minutes with only the sound of the wipers and his own breathing as a wall between himself and the night. The road is broken here, asphalt cracked and the shoulder washed away to rock and clay, and sickly undergrowth giving way to sparse woodland that has been shredded by foot traffic. Even inside the car he can smell damp earth and leaf mold, the faintly saline reek of Seattle rain pooling alongside the cracked road. He drives carefully, slowly, telling himself it's because the road is so bad, if he drives any faster he'll lose a hubcap. He tells himself it is because he is in no hurry to get home. He tells himself many things, and keeps his hands very, very tight upon the wheel.

There is a spot where the road curves,

where for one last instant the night is simple darkness. That's when his heart begins to pound. Not fast, not at first; slowly, but hard enough it feels as though someone is shoving a fist against his chest. He takes a deep breath, fighting what feels like panic, but he knows it is something else, knows it has a name, but he can't hear it; the wall is there, and he will never hear what they say behind it, what they call it, what they would call him if they knew. His breath comes harder and he fights it, fights to keep his fingers rigid upon the steering wheel. Because this time he isn't going to stop. This time he will keep going, his foot will tap the accelerator and the dark sedan will jounce past and he won't stop, he won't stop until he's home.

He drives around the curve, and there before him is the stretch of road, the darkness soiled now by the first red eyes of taillights watching him. His foot hovers above the gas pedal, and the sedan floats on, rain silvering the windshield, the road beneath him like water now, and he moves without a sound, he is behind the wall, and they can't hear him. Clouds of exhaust rise from the shattered asphalt; he tugs at his baseball cap, as though to shield himself from poisonous fumes. In the near distance rears the bridge he has just crossed, its immense supporting piers devoured by shadow and trees, its span lost to shrouded fog. As he gazes at it his breath quickens: he blinks, loosening his hold upon the steering wheel for just an instant as he struggles to keep the wall in place, fights not to see what is moving in the darkness. He will not go there, will not go there . . .

For the moment, the wall holds.

On the road's right shoulder cars begin to appear through the mist. Some of them are empty. Many are not: he can see the silhouettes of men sitting and talking, or embracing, the sickening stigmatic flash of a head bobbing quickly, up and down. His breathing grows louder; within his chest his heart aches as though he has been stabbed, as though they are heaving stones at him. He opens his mouth and gasps, the breath leaving him and freezing into a soundless howl. Because the wall is crumbling now. He can feel it, slabs of darkness crashing against his breast and the taste it leaves in his mouth, like biting into metal until his gums bleed. Outside shadowy figures move slowly through the mist. There is the muted slam of car doors opening and closing. He shakes his head, frantic, trying to find the accelerator, but his foot is numb, he can no longer feel the wheel beneath his hands or his heart beating or even the sough of air within his throat—because that is what the wall does when it crumbles, its weight crushes you and how can you feel anything, how can you expect a man to feel anything at all, beneath that terrible weight?

"Hey. . . . ."

A voice echoes thickly, he has a glimpse of a white face turning to watch him pass. With a cry he looks away and leans hard against the steering wheel, trying to force himself to feel it there. Because he is going, he is going to drive straight home, he has taken a wrong turn, he has taken a shortcut, he has only come here to look . . .

That is how it always starts. And the taste in his mouth as he slows the car to a crawl and, for the first time, very slowly and deliberately turns to look out at the figures moving through the trees—the taste of blood and earth and semen, the taste of stone where the wall gives way—that is how it starts, too.

And that is how it always ends.

He parks. Some distance from the other cars, though not so far as to draw any attention to himself. Soon enough there will be other cars beside his. For a few minutes he sits there in the darkness. He can hear the wind, wailing softly where his window is cracked open, the rattle of branches and low laughter from the edge of the woods. Another car creeps up beside his, pauses long enough for him to see the flash of a face behind glass, questioning eyes. He sucks his breath in and looks away, staring unblinkingly into the rearview mirror, seeing nothing. After a moment the other car drives past. He waits until it is out of sight, tugging his baseball cap snugly against his forehead. Then he gets out and heads into the woods.

Susurrus of voices, dead leaves, distant traffic. The ground beneath his feet is spongy. Each step releases something from the earth: foul gases, an odor of decay, pallid mushrooms like fingertips thrusting through the mold. The air against his face feels viscous, and carries with it the smell of spoiled meat. He blinks, striving to see through a mist that is more like some thick liquid, grayish and rent with darker gashes, black and umber, dull red like blood flaking from a scab. The trees move slowly in a breeze that reeks of ammonia and formaldehyde. Their branches trace words in the air and his eyes water as without stopping he reads them, his lips move though he does not speak the words aloud—

'Tis now the very witching time of
  night,
When churchyards yawn and hell itself
  breathes out
Contagion to this world . . .

They are there now, he can see them:
walking between desiccated saplings at the
base of the bridge, fog roiling about their legs.
Eyes like burned-out candles, black and edged
with crimson, faces pocked with earth and the
fragile tracery of decay: flesh peeling into
bloody lace, minute creatures scuttling across
their cheeks. Their mouths are sewn shut, the
stitches dead black against bloodless skin.
Some have their eyes sewn shut as well,
threads drawn taut where they struggle to open
them, their arms outstretched as they stagger
sightless through the forest. Rhododendrons
claw at them, leaves slashing at exposed ten-
dons, the blackened knob of an arm from
which the hand has been severed at the wrist.
Despite their shuttered mouths he can hear
them, liquescent sobs as they fall to their
knees and couple there in the raw earth, eyeless, mouthless, thrusting like maggots burying
themselves in the soil. Where they lie small
gouts of flame erupt from the ground and blaze
about the bodies: but the corpses continue

their coupling, heedless. He stops, bracing himself against a tree as he gasps and tries desperately not to see them or hear them, tries desperately to see the wall there between himself and the dead men beneath the bridge.

And slowly, slowly, it works. Stone by stone, shadow by shadow, the wall rises before him. The flames licking at the corners of his eyes die back; the legless shapes humping along the ground fade into rocks and stands of alder. The whispering voices fade as well, though he knows they are still there; just as he knows the men are still there, walking quickly along the well-worn paths leading beneath the bridge. But for the moment he cannot see them, not really; for the moment the wall holds. He turns and stumbles back to his car, crashing heedlessly through bushes and sending stones flying beneath his feet. He is dimly aware of startled faces turning from him, and once a cautious hand reaching for his. He hears the low admonishment, "Hey, chill, man, it's okay, it's okay—" and then a low whistle, someone pronouncing, "Looks like he saw a fucking ghost—"

—and then he is back on the road, cracked tarmac under his shoes and the woods receding behind him into blessed darkness. A few yards ahead of him is his car: he can reach it, get inside and turn the ignition, turn the wheel, turn from all this and in half an hour he will be home, it will never happen again, it will be over, finally it will all be over . . .

He reaches the car. Unlocks it and slides inside, the door slamming behind him with a hollow rattle. His heart roars in his chest and his breathing comes fast and shallow. Nausea clutches at his insides. He is going to pass out. He leans forward until his forehead touches the steering wheel, sits there and takes deep breaths, forcing himself to exhale slowly, to keep the wall from crumbling. After a few minutes his breathing grows more even; his heart pounds, but he can count the space between each beat; it is getting better. Carefully he brings his hands up to the wheel, thinking *I can do this, I can do this, it is time to go*; when suddenly there is a rap at the window.

He jumps, drawing back so hard his knees bang against the lower edge of the wheel. The rap comes again, more insistent this time. Very slowly he turns and gazes at the passenger window. A young man's face is framed there, dark hair close-cropped and flannel shirt casually unbuttoned inside a suede windbreaker pearled with moisture. The young man cocks his head and stares at him, after a moment tentatively smiles: a reassuring smile, *Hey chill man, it's okay, it's okay* . . .

The Frenchman stares back. All around him he hears soft thunder, stones tumbling from an unimaginable height. Between himself and the window small patches of darkness bloom, and within one of these he sees the young man's face, mouth no longer smiling because of what is there between his lips, eyes no longer looking upon the man in the car because catgut has been threaded between the upper and lower lids. On the front of his suede windbreaker blood pearls in tiny droplets, forming a stream that courses down to his chest, down the opening of the young man's flannel shirt until it soaks his chest.

From very far away he hears a noise, the grating sound of the car's passenger door opening and then slamming shut. But he does not hear the door close: in the Frenchman's ears the thunder is deafening now. It is the sound of the wall falling away, it is the sound of waves upon a shore, of the crimson tide rising, rising, until the city drowns beneath it. It is the sound of the world ending, not with a bang, not with a whimper, but with the dull throb of a car engine revving up, the crunch of gravel beneath its wheels as its headlights slice through the shrouded mist and the dark sedan pulls away from the bridge.

MILLENNIUM
CHAPTER

8

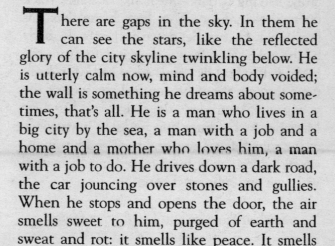

There are gaps in the sky. In them he can see the stars, like the reflected glory of the city skyline twinkling below. He is utterly calm now, mind and body voided; the wall is something he dreams about sometimes, that's all. He is a man who lives in a big city by the sea, a man with a job and a home and a mother who loves him, a man with a job to do. He drives down a dark road, the car jouncing over stones and gullies. When he stops and opens the door, the air smells sweet to him, purged of earth and sweat and rot: it smells like peace. It smells like the sea. He stands there for a moment, just breathing. Thinking, *I love this city*; thinking how good it is, to be able to save something you love. From far away drifts the murmur of traffic, the hoot of a car ferry drawing up to the main terminal just north of Pioneer Square. It is a sound he loves, now. Once again it is a world he can live in.

He walks to the passenger side of the car and opens it. Something moves inside, so that for an instant he freezes: a body, tumbling with exquisite slowness from the passenger seat out onto the ground at his feet. It leans there awkwardly, one arm splayed up against the open door. The open palm rests there, then slides away, leaving a dark smear like a snail's track upon the interior. The Frenchman lets his breath out. He reaches down and grabs the body by the ankles and begins dragging it toward the back of the car. His hands are sheathed in latex now; through them he can feel the spur of the young man's ankles, the edges of his Doc Martens. As he drags him he looks impassively at the ruined face, eyes and nose and lips indistinguishable now, a huge ragged mouth matted with hair and splintered bone.

So shalt thou feed on Death, that feeds
on men,

> *And Death once dead, there's no more*
> *dying then . . .*

When he reaches the back of the car he works quickly, dropping the body and unlocking the trunk. Inside it is lined, very neatly, with heavy visqueen plastic. He stoops and hefts the body once again, grunting softly as he angles it, until at last, with a muted thud, it falls to the bottom of the trunk. For a long moment he stares down at it, tugging absently at the bill of his baseball cap, then closes the lid. Quickly he crosses back to the front of the car, gets in, and drives off. It is almost sunrise, and he has work to do.

It is a huge responsibility at the end of the world, to save a dying city from damnation.

MILLENNIUM
CHAPTER

9

Morning dawned jewel-bright, sunlight touching the beveled windows of Frank's bedroom and turning them into prisms. He lay on his side in bed, watching the rainbows dart across the floor as outside the windows trees moved in a soft breeze. Behind him Catherine lay with the comforter pulled up to her chin, eyes closed but smiling: she was pretending to be asleep. In front of him Jordan sat cross-legged atop the comforter, frowning seriously as she looked at the classifieds section of yesterday's paper. From outside came the familiar whoosh of bicycles speeding past, the cheerful jingle of their old-fashioned bells momentarily drowning out birdsong, a neighbor whistling as she clipped her hedgerow.

"What's a boxer?"

Frank looked up, smiling, into his daughter's puzzled face. "A big dog with a face like this," he whispered—picking out a puppy was supposed to be a secret from Catherine—and contorted his features into an admirable semblance of a very ugly canine. Jordan studied him, brow furrowed, and finally shook her head.

"I don't think so," she said, and went back to the classifieds.

Catherine's smile broadened. She shook her head—did anyone *ever* really keep a secret from Mom? *Ever?*

"What about a basset hound?" she suggested.

Jordan stared guiltily at her father: Uh-oh. Busted by Mom. Still, she waited expectantly for him to weigh in on basset hounds.

"Nope," he said, grinning as he leaned back to gaze at his wife. "Too many big ears in this house already."

Catherine sat up and gave him her best Edward G. Robinson tough-guy glare.

"Now we know why Daddy has a face like a boxer."

Jordan collapsed into giggles. The classifieds crinkled noisily as her mother reached over and grabbed her in a hug. "What are you two up to—" she began, when the morning's peace was broken by the telephone's shrill bleating.

Frank answered it. "Hello?"

"Frank." The voice on the other end sounded hollow and staticky: someone on a portable. "It's Bob Bletcher. We found a body. I think you might want to come take a look."

In one smooth motion Frank swung around, sitting on the edge of the bed beside the nightstand. He could feel Catherine's eyes boring into him as he said in a low voice, "Yeah. I think so."

"Off 90, down by the Snoqualmie." Bletcher's words grew faint as the connection faded. "You'll see the circus—"

"Right. See you out there," said Frank. The line went dead, and he sat up as he replaced the phone.

On the bed behind him Catherine stared at him curiously. "Who was that?"

Frank sat for a moment before answering. "Bob Bletcher," he said at last. "He wants me to look at something for him."

Catherine tried to keep the edge from her voice. "What?"

"It's just a favor." He turned and gazed into her eyes, held them as he shook his head very slightly, indicating Jordan. Catherine bit her lip, nodding, as Frank reached to tousle Jordan's hair. "We'll finish up later, okay, sweetie?" he said, and kissed her forehead. Jordan grinned.

"Sure, Daddy."

For a long moment he stood there, looking at Jordan. He remembered being in the hospital with his wife after she had gone into labor: the long hours of waiting, ending with the miracle he and Catherine had never expected to see—their infant daughter held triumphantly in the arms of the nurse-midwife, and minutes later gently put into her mother's arms. The pregnancy had been difficult, but nothing had been worse than the years that preceded it, when specialist after specialist had told them a child would be impossible to conceive, and all the test results bore their words out.

But the specialists had been wrong. He watched Jordan now as here head dipped and she began once again to read the classifieds. The doctors had been wrong, and Jordan was proof: their miracle, their one-in-a-million chance, their winning ticket.

And nothing could change that. Nothing would ever take her away from them.

He shook his head, quickly, blinking at the sudden wave of emotion that overcame him. He crossed the room, stooping to gather up the rest of the scattered newspaper as he made his way to his dresser. With one hand he pulled the drawer open, started rummaging for socks and underwear. With the other hand he started to toss the paper onto a bureau, when the front page caught his eye.

SUSPECT SOUGHT IN
STRIP CLUB SLAYING

There was another overexposed photograph of Calamity, and beneath that the words:

Forensic evidence points to
a black male, possibly . . .

He gathered his clothes and shoved the paper under his arm. "I'll be home for dinner," he called over his shoulder as he hurried into the bathroom to get dressed.

MILLENNIUM
CHAPTER
10

He drove east on Interstate 90, heading toward the Snoqualmie River. If you followed the river north, toward the Cascades, you'd find Snoqualmie Falls, a spectacular crescendo of white water with its famous lodge overlooking the chilly, rainbow-studded spray. If you followed the highway long enough, it would take you across the entire country. But Frank didn't need to go that far, not today.

It was easy to find the murder site. About twenty miles out of town, where police cars and ambulances angled across the shoulder and onto the dead grass. Beyond was a broad, barren slope of land leading down to the river, thinly wooded with birches and young oaks, their gray limbs leafless, scratching fretfully at a heavy sky the color of a gunpowder burn. Frank parked his Cherokee where the road ended and began walking toward the incline. Frozen moss gave a brittle crunch beneath his tread; there was the dull gleam of frost on dead leaves and tree trunks. Where the hill widened, unfolding into the river basin, several dozen uniformed officers and search-and-rescue personnel combed the frozen ground. Somewhere out of sight a helicopter droned. There was the twittering of walkie-talkies and portable phones, an occasional blast from a transmitter broadcasting from the helicopter, the muted din of conversations and shouted commands, excited whines and barking from the K–9 corps straining at their leashes. Frank took it all in, but before he could start down the hill a uniformed officer came panting up to him.

"Sorry, sir, but this area is closed except to authorized—"

"It's okay, Officer." Bletcher's voice rang out over the clamor. "He's here at my request—" The officer turned away as Bletcher joined Frank. "It looks like I called you out here a little hastily." Bletcher tilted his head, indicating that Frank should follow him downhill.

"What is it?"

"A body. Male." Bletcher emphasized the word, glancing sideways at Frank as he added, "It was charred so badly we couldn't tell the sex at first."

Frank hesitated, staring down to where a knot of uniformed officers and detectives stood in a loose circle around a tarpaulin. "Somebody set it on fire?"

Bletcher nodded and restlessly tapped his walkie-talkie against his side. Years of this sort of thing had taken the edge from his voice when discussing the daily horrors of his job, but still he couldn't keep the disgust from showing. "Either before or after it had been decapitated. We can't tell yet."

Frank looked at him, taking in the lines drawn tight around Bletcher's mouth, the smudged circles beneath his eyes. Then he brought his attention back to the group at the bottom of the hill. He recognized Giebelhouse and the other detectives from Bletcher's office. As their boss approached with Frank they grew silent, eyes cold as they stared at the newcomer. Corpses and brutality were endured as part of the job. Interlopers were not. Frank edged past, not even noticing their icily detached expressions, the ironic cast of professional jealousy warring with genuine curiosity. Frank ignored them. His gaze was fixed on the body beneath the tarp.

"Has it been touched or moved?" he asked.

Bletcher shook his head. The walkie-talkie crackled, and he turned it down. "No."

Frank swiveled his head, looking past the circle of dark-clad men. His gaze flickered restlessly from one barren copse to the next, skirting a washed-out gully, stones heaped at the base of an immense fallen tree.

At the very corners of his vision phantom shapes pulse and retreat, teasingly.

"It looks like whoever killed him did it somewhere else, then brought him out here," Bletcher went on. "He must've parked on the road up top, pushed him down the hill."

Frank nodded, hardly hearing him. A few feet away Giebelhouse lifted his head and called out in a grudging tone, "You probably want to see the body."

Frank's eyes narrowed, staring at a spot between ragged-looking saplings. "No, that's okay," he said, and, without warning, he began to lope toward the trees.

"Frank—" Bletcher called.

Frank says nothing. He moves as though

entranced, not feeling where branches whip against his hands and face, heedless of the icy damp seeping into his shoes. The softly pulsing shapes swim across his field of vision. In his mouth there is the taste of blood and dirt, a fleck of something soft and damp as a bit of torn tissue. The sky overhead pales from pewter to silver. There is a pink glow on the eastern horizon. Dawn; but the glow grows too bright too fast, not dawn at all, but flames. Through the trees a figure staggers, black and writhing like a mayfly caught in a candle's blaze, flame spurting from its flailing arms and head. Frank inhales sharply, almost gags on the stench of burning hair, roasting flesh. An inhuman voice is screaming, the crackling of the flames nearly drowning anguished shrieks, the glottal moans of someone trying to scream even as his tongue is seared to ash. All around him the landscape melts into black and crimson, trees and brush bursting into flame. Shadowy forms drag themselves across the ground, eyeless, mouthless. The odor of burning sickens him, he wants to wrench his eyes away but cannot: the burning man is running at him, sparks and motes of ash spinning from him like fireflies. Within the inferno that was his face Frank can see his eyes, twin rows of tiny red-streaked X's where they have been sewn shut, and the melting horror that was a mouth, its stitches turned to flame.

"Frank . . ." Bletcher's voice was a thread of light curling through that darkness. "Can you—"

Frank says nothing: because now he sees another figure, one that stands half-hidden behind two trees, its hands hanging limply at its sides. A man in jeans and dark jacket, a baseball cap obscuring his face.

"Frank?"

"It's the same killer."

"*What?*"

Frank blinked, focusing on Bletcher's confused expression. "He did it here." As he spoke the vision faded. The reek of burning gave way to the chill scent of rain on stone, the horrific screams grew faint as the search helicopter roared directly overhead. Frank breathed in and out quickly, as though testing the air, then looked down. "The victim was set afire here in the woods."

He began to walk, fast, kicking at leaves as he hurried down the slope looking for traces of burning—charred leaves or cloth, white ash. "How far to the river?" he called back to Bletcher.

The chief detective strode after him. "A quarter mile."

Frank's voice rang out clearly above the helicopter. "That's where they came from."

Bletcher paused, staring after him.

"Who's this guy think he is?" called out one of the detectives. "Sherlock Holmes?"

"I dunno," muttered Bletcher. "I guess we'll find out."

He raced down the hill after Frank. Behind him he heard his men grumbling, then calling out to each other as they prepared to follow. There was a burst of static from his walkie-talkie, and then a staticky voice: the helicopter feed.

"This is air mobile one to base. Yeah, we've got what could be something down near the river."

"Right," Bletcher said grimly, setting off again.

He found Frank near the river's edge. The thick carpet of leaves there had been disturbed: foot-shaped impressions in the leaves, some solid prints in the black humus beneath. A little farther on, signs of a scuffle—upturned stones, broken mushrooms, more scattered leaves. Frank stood in the middle of it, scrutinizing the ground and surrounding brush.

"They were down here," he said.

Bletcher came up beside him, panting slightly. "Doing what, though?"

A frown creased the other man's gaunt face. "I'm not sure."

Bletcher shrugged. "Then why—"

"OVER HERE!"

The two men turned to see Giebelhouse and Detective Kamm beckoning them urgently from behind a clump of birches. At their feet two uniformed officers were digging furiously at the leaves. Frank sprinted toward them, Bletcher at his side.

"This is it," one of the officers announced, then swore. Frank and Bletcher drew up beside the other detectives, looked down to see what the officers had uncovered.

A coffin. Crudely made of unfinished wood, splinters feathering up where the nails had been hastily hammered in. On its top a word had been scratched into the wood, the letters uneven and clumsily formed.

PESTE

Frank watched as the men cleared away the leaves, searching frantically for the edges of the lid. The smell of mold grew stronger, and he shook his head. His throat ached, and his eyes. The warmth at the base of his skull was gone: he felt locked in ice.

"It's empty." His voice was numb.

A moment later one of the officers cried out as he found the edges of the buried rectangle. There was the *skreek* of nails and wood giving way as they prised the lid from the coffin. And found—

Nothing. A few dead leaves sifted to the bottom as the officers knelt and stared inside. Nothing at all; save a rust-colored stain in one corner.

"Look."

One of the officers pointed at the interior lid, and the others stared silently at what was there. A broken series of gouges in the rough wood, streaked with reddish brown: the marks left where someone had tried to claw his way out.

"Shit." Bletcher swore beneath his breath. When he looked up again, he saw Frank walking away. Without a word to the others Bletcher hurried to catch up with him.

"I think we should have a talk."

Frank said nothing. They walked the rest of the way in silence until they reached Frank's Cherokee. Bletcher waited as the other man opened the driver's door and stepped inside. He sat beside the wheel, staring wordlessly at the chief detective. Finally, as the helicopter's drone grew louder and more voices echoed up to them from the river, Frank nodded.

"Get in," he said. "I'll take you back downtown."

They drove without speaking, through the blasted winter countryside at the outskirts of town and on into the heart of the city. When they reached downtown it was raining again. Traffic slowed to its familiar midday crawl. Frank turned on the radio, fiddling with the dial until he found a classical station. Bletcher watched him as he sat impassively behind the wheel, staring out at the lines of cars in front of them, the wipers sweeping rhythmically back and forth, back and forth. Finally the detective reached over and turned the radio down.

"Your associate was down in Pathology looking at the body this morning," he said. "A guy named Watts."

Frank registered the name, shrugged noncommittally. "I haven't spoken to him yet."

"A couple of my detectives did. He told them he was part of something called the Millennium Group."

Frank still refused to meet his gaze. "Yeah."

But Bletcher refused to be put off. "Is that who you're doing this consulting for?"

"Uh-huh."

The detective opened his hands, stared at

his palms, then out at the driving rain. "So who are they?"

Frank's tone was measured, almost casual. "Just some guys who used to work in law enforcement."

"FBI?"

"Some of them."

Bletcher studied him. He'd known Frank Black long enough to recognize when he was withholding something. But he'd also known him long enough to realize that nothing, not threats or pleading or deliberate nonchalance, would induce Frank to talk if he didn't want to. Ahead of them traffic began to move toward the intersection where the County Courts Building loomed through the pouring rain. The Cherokee inched forward. Bletcher finally sighed, shaking his head. His tone rose slightly; like it or not, he was pleading.

"My guys want to know why you're here. I still don't know what to tell them."

Frank reached for the radio and pressed the volume button. The Kronos Quartet filled the Cherokee. George Crumb's "Black Angels." They halted again at another light, and he turned to Bletcher. His gaze was unguarded, and, like Bletcher's, his voice held a note of entreaty. "I'm here because I have a wife and a kid, and I want to raise them in a place they can feel safe."

Bletcher waited to hear if there was more. When there was not, he said, "That's it?"

Frank nodded and turned to stare out at the rain, the army of black umbrellas massed upon the sidewalk. Bletcher took a deep breath, then softly asked, "You want to talk about what happened? Why you quit the bureau?"

"No."

Abruptly the Cherokee lurched forward, pulling over to the curb in front of the Courts Building. Bletcher sighed, lips pressed tightly together, and opened his door. He got out, but before he shut the door he stuck his head back in again.

"How do you do it, Frank?"

Frank's cool eyes met his. "Lucky guesser."

Bletcher stared back at him, frowning. A moment later the passenger door slammed, and Frank watched dispassionately as the detective sprinted through the rain to shelter.

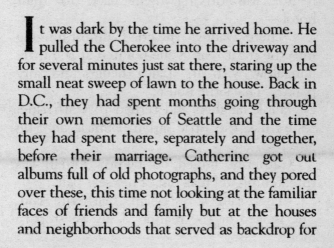

It was dark by the time he arrived home. He pulled the Cherokee into the driveway and for several minutes just sat there, staring up the small neat sweep of lawn to the house. Back in D.C., they had spent months going through their own memories of Seattle and the time they had spent there, separately and together, before their marriage. Catherine got out albums full of old photographs, and they pored over these, this time not looking at the familiar faces of friends and family but at the houses and neighborhoods that served as backdrop for all those snapshots of weddings, backyard barbecues, surprise parties, bridal showers, softball games, and the Strawberry Festival on Vashon Island. Modest, gentrified homes on Capitol Hill; postmodern mansions hidden in the firs overlooking Lake Washington; newer homes along the north side of Green Lake. They had made one trip back, with Jordan, to look actively for a place to live—two weeks of poring through the classifieds and riding around with realtors, checking faucets and basements for signs of damp, thumping on Sheetrock and scratching at wooden floors in search of dry rot.

This house hadn't even been on their list. Jordan had spotted it one afternoon when a realtor was driving them back to their hotel—

"There, Daddy!" she cried, almost lunging into the front seat as she pointed at the little bungalow with its azalea hedge and airy porch. "That's the house!"

Frank laughed and turned to Catherine. "She's like the little girl in *Miracle on 34th Street*."

Catherine smiled, but by now Jordan was threatening to break out of her seat belt.

"There's a FOR SALE sign," Catherine said. She looked at the realtor. "Can we stop to look?"

The realtor looked doubtful. "It's not our listing," she began, but at sight of three excited pairs of eyes she nodded. "But we can look around outside now, and I'll see what I can do."

They went back the next day, and the next. That afternoon they made an offer. The house had been brown then, the window shutters a peeling gray-green, but from the first Jordan and Catherine had known it would be yellow.

"It wants to be yellow," Jordan insisted.

"Can't argue with a house," Frank admitted. So once back in D.C. there were not only the hours spent packing but still more hours staring at paint samples. Sunflower Yellow, Paris Morning, Citron Dream, Wheat. Who knew there were so many different shades of yellow? But at last Catherine and Jordan made up their minds: One Foot in Eden Yellow, Benjamin Moore Latex Semi-Gloss, with bright white trim.

Now, sitting in the Cherokee, Frank smiled. In the mellow light from the street lamp, the little house fairly glowed. Moths fluttered around the porch light. One of the upstairs bedroom windows gleamed faint gold, its beveled panes like the spun-sugar windows of a gingerbread house.

It may not be exactly one foot in Eden, he thought, *but it's certainly a toe in the door.* He got out and started up the walk. He was almost at the front steps when the sound of a car door slamming stopped him.

"Frank Black . . . ?"

He froze, his hands unconsciously curling into fists as he turned. On the far side of the road a car was parked beneath the streetlight. A man stepped from it and strode confidently across the street and up the walk toward Frank.

"Yes?" Frank waited.

As he drew closer the man's features became clear. Tall and muscular, about Frank's age, with a shaven head and mustache, wearing a Burberry raincoat and chinos; shoes that, like his coat, were expensive but nondescript. Everything about him—clothes, chiseled features, forthright gaze—exuded assurance, and power.

"I'm Peter Watts." His voice was low and beautifully modulated, utterly self-possessed. "From the group. I would have faxed you, but I wanted to introduce myself."

Frank relaxed, allowing himself a cordial smile, and extended his hand. "I'd heard you were down looking at the body. Did you find anything?"

Watts held out a manila envelope. "A few things that slipped by. One salient oversight—"

"Frank?"

The two men turned, to see Catherine standing in the open front door of the house. The porch light made a dark aureole of her hair, and one held closed the collar of her white bathrobe. Frank gave her a reassuring nod.

"I'll be right in, Catherine."

She remained in the doorway for a moment, as though waiting for an explanation. When none came she tipped her head and shut the door. Watts waited until her shadow could be seen in the living-room window, and went on.

"There was severe blunt trauma to the body, so it was easy to miss. On the inside of the victim's left thigh I found a needle puncture."

Frank raised his eyebrows. "From what? A syringe?"

"Maybe. There was no evidence of anything administered in the adipose of surrounding tissue." He hesitated, then said, "I know they think the killer is a black male, but—"

Frank nodded, staring intently at the other man's face. "I've already ruled that out."

Watts met his gaze, shot him a tight smile of agreement. Frank felt a small surge of pride.

"The severance of the head and fingers was done with skill and precision." Watts waited as Frank took the envelope from him, glancing at it. "You know why—"

Frank tapped the envelope against his hand. "The killer was covering his tracks. The victim may have scratched or bitten him. He may not have gone there to kill her."

Watts agreed. "The kitchen knife was convenient, that's all. But even with something that clumsy, he knew what he was doing. And he did it with real sangfroid, judging from his tidy cleanup."

Frank nodded again with grim satisfaction. "What does the group think?"

"That your instincts are right. The killer is being compelled by an extraneous stressor. He's out of control."

"Anything else?"

Watts smiled: he looked like nothing so much as the revered head coach, welcoming a new star player to the team. "That you're the right man for the job. And a fine addition to the group. All our resources are available to you."

Frank inclined his head, acknowledging

the unspoken congratulation in the other man's words. Watts raised a hand in farewell, turned, and headed back to his car. Frank watched him go, giving Watts a subdued wave as his car eased back out onto the main road. Then he went inside, stooping to pick up that morning's paper, still wrapped in plastic against the rain.

The house was dark. He made his way carefully through the front hall—there were still empty boxes waiting to be taken to the recycling center—and walked toward the kitchen. The sweet smell of cinnamon sugar overpowered that of fresh paint and wood shavings. Frank smiled, recalling how that morning before school Jordan had pleaded with her mother to make snickerdoodles.

And sure enough, there they were on the counter, carefully mounded beneath plastic wrap. He set the newspaper on the counter, lifted the edge of the plastic wrap, took a cookie, and ate it in two bites; then he took another, for good measure, poured himself a glass of milk, and stood for a few minutes by the sink, gazing out toward the neighbor's yard. What was his name? Meredith—Jack Meredith. Seemed like an okay guy. Maybe he had grand-kids Jordan's age. That would be nice. He'd have to remember to ask Catherine if she'd spoken to Meredith or his wife, to make plans to see them for dinner. He finished his milk, set the glass in the sink, hooked one more cookie for the road, and headed up to bed.

The light was out when he got there. Catherine was in bed beneath the comforter, facing away from him. Her curling hair spilled across the pillow in dark coils. For a moment he stood in the doorway, listening for Catherine's even breathing, wondering if she was already asleep.

But no. "Who was that?" she asked. She did not turn to look at him.

Frank took a deep breath, tucked the manila envelope up under his arm. "His name is Watts. He had some information for me."

"He sat out there for an hour. He could have come to the door."

Frank made a helpless gesture. "I don't think he wanted to impose."

Catherine sat up in bed, the covers falling away from her. "I can handle imposition, Frank," she said. Her voice was strained, but not angry: this was not a new topic. "What I can't handle is secrecy."

Her husband crossed the room and sat on the bed beside her. "I don't keep secrets, Catherine. I'll tell you anything you want. You know that."

"You think you're protecting me. But you make it worse, Frank." She shook her head, but there was still no anger in her tone. "You can't shut the world out for me. You can't ask me to pretend I don't know what you do."

Frank reached over to place the envelope on the nightstand, then leaned back. He stroked Catherine's arm gently. "Everyone pretends. We all make believe. These men I catch—they make us."

Catherine shook her head. "We're raising a daughter, Frank. The real world starts to seep in. You can't stop it."

He pulled her to him, gently, and kissed her forehead. "I want you to make believe that I can."

For a moment Catherine gazed at him, her dark eyes thoughtful; then she leaned into his embrace, let him hold her tightly as his mouth found hers.

And for a little while, they really did make believe that the world wasn't there.

M uch later he lay still abed, wide-awake beside his wife. Catherine's breathing was slow and even. For the moment, at least, there was no need to pretend that she was at peace. He remained there, listening to her; finally sighed: sleep would not come. He kissed her cheek, tucking the comforter around her shoulders, and got up.

In Jordan's room his daughter was sprawled across her mattress, a smaller, untidier version of her mother. Frank watched her for several minutes, holding his own breath so that he could hear hers—habit borne of long anxiety, too many nights without sleep, nights that had seemed to be without dawn. After a minute he turned, reluctantly, reaching for the nightstand and the manila envelope he had left there. He went downstairs.

The house was so still he could hear the clock ticking in the living room, the soft creaking of boards settling on the stair risers. He returned to the kitchen for a few more cookies, got himself a drink from the refrigerator. Then he grabbed that morning's paper, sliding off its plastic wrapper and glancing at the headlines as he headed for the basement.

A dehumidifier hummed softly in one corner, the new boiler gurgled to itself in another. In between—an unfinished wall of two-by-fours marking out where, someday, the boundaries of his office would be—Frank had set up temporary headquarters. A large square of old, unwanted carpeting from upstairs covered the bare concrete floor. There was a sprung-bottomed upholstered chair, several tables holding support equipment—printers, fax machines, lamps, telephone, television, VCR. A set of bookshelves holding several dictionaries, a thesaurus, *Physician's Desk Reference*, and other books. A bulletin board, nailed to the two-by-fours, and holding thumbtacked Polaroids and newspaper clippings relating to Calamity's murder. Atop a lovingly restored Mission oak desk sat Frank's computer, its screen glowing a neutral steel blue. Beside it was a digital scanner and Mavigraph video grab. Frank picked up his reading glasses where he'd left them beside the monitor. He swept aside some stray papers, replaced them with the envelope Peter Watts had given him, and swung into his chair, grabbing his mouse and clicking on an icon. A small box appeared in the center of the screen, enclosing shimmering letters.

CONNECTING TO MILLENNIUM GROUP.

There was a series of beeps and the hissing squeal of the modem dialing and then connecting. Once he was sure it had made contact, Frank picked up the manila envelope and carefully opened it, spilling its contents onto the desk. Photos, an audiocassette, a videotape, faxes, and several pages of typed notes. Frank glanced at these, then turned back to the computer screen when it beeped. The screen was empty, save for the words

HELLO, FRANK.

He stood, taking the videotape Watts had given him, and put it into the VCR. Turned his chair so that he could watch the monitor, a pad of legal paper balanced on his lap, VCR remote in one hand and a pen in the other. There was a flicker of gray and white across the video screen. Grainy black-and-white images appeared. Frank frowned: the resolution was so bad, it took him a moment to get his bearings.

But here it was: the interior of the private booth at The Ruby Tip. Viewed from above, at a wide angle—from the surveillance camera. To the right of the screen was a dully gleaming slant of light that was the glass window; behind it a dark figure could just barely be glimpsed, her seductive movements smelted down to a few stray background flickers. Most of the screen was taken up by a larger shadow, close to the glass. The silhouette of a man in profile, his features all but obscured by a baseball cap. The audio blared a pounding hard-core song, but beneath its insistent beat Frank could make out another sound—a man's voice, whispering, his tone urgent though the words were garbled.

Frank leaned forward, until he was only inches from the screen, rewound the tape, and played it back. Listening even more intently than he had the first time, studying the oblique shadow of the man's face, the black slit that was his mouth as he whispered to the woman

behind the glass. Frank's eyes remained fixed
on the TV. His hand moved quickly across the
notepad in his lap, transcribing words.

He rewound it again, and again, copying
out more phrases, crossing them out and
entering new ones—

BLOOD RIMMED TIDE
BLOOD DIMMED TIDE
WHERE THE AIR AND MONEY OF
    INNOCENCE
WHERE THE CEREMONY OF
    INNOCENCE IS DROWN
IS DROWNED

He rubbed his eyes, squinting as he played
back the tape for the dozenth time. And
copied out the words more slowly this time as
they began to echo what he was hearing on
the monitor.

WHERE THE CEREMONY OF
    INNOCENCE IS DROWNED

"... *everywhere, the ceremony of innocence* . . ."
He stopped. Stopped the tape, stopped
writing. The phrase tugged at his memory: he
bit his lip, brow furrowed, then turned to the
neat shelf of reference books and pulled down

Bartlett's Familiar Quotations. He turned to
the back of the thick volume, riffling through
pages until he found what he was looking for.

> Ceremony, distinctions by means
> of c., 101a
>   idol c., 244b
>   known as afternoon tea, 798a
>   love useth enforced c., 256a
>   of innocence drowned, 882a

Excitedly he flipped back to page 882. And
there it was—Yeats's "The Second Coming,"
half-remembered from college English classes—

> *Turning and turning in the widening*
>   *gyre*
> *The falcon cannot hear the falconer;*
> *Things fall apart; the center cannot*
>   *hold;*
> *Mere anarchy is loosed upon the*
>   *world,*
> *The blood-dimmed tide is loosed, and*
> *everywhere*
> *The ceremony of innocence is*
>   *drowned . . .*

He scanned through the rest of the verse,
until he reached its final lines.

And what rough beast, its hour come
   round at last,
Slouches towards Bethlehem to be
   born?

"That's it," he whispered.

"*The great plague in the maritime city,*" the enhanced voice cried hoarsely. "*You'll have your part in the lake which burns with fire and brimstone . . .*"

He closed the book, looked up at the bulletin board with its gruesome gallery of Polaroids. Crime-scene photos, showing discrete parts of Calamity's battered body, the crook of leg, handless arms crossed upon a bloodied torso, hanks of hair. Three photos lined up side by side by side: close-ups of a pale unidentifiable expanse of skin, the anonymous flesh bruised and scabbed with blood. Only in the third picture was anything else indicated, by a circle drawn in red grease pencil. In its center Frank could clearly discern a tiny black spot.

On the inside of the victim's left thigh I found a needle puncture . . .

He turned excitedly from the Polaroid, back to the VCR. Pointed the remote and set the videotape rolling again. As he listened to the garbled transmission he took a small stack of Polaroids from beside the keyboard and flipped through them yet again, half-hoping that this time there would be something there he had not seen already, something besides blood and charred flesh. *". . . the great plague in the maritime city,"* a voice was intoning harshly from the TV. *"You'll have your part in the lake which burns with fire and brimstone."*

He reached the bottom of the little pile of Polaroids. Several police photos of the crime scene he had visited that morning. Churned-up leaves, footprints, several sepia-tinged images of the buried coffin and its lid, the word etched there like a warning.

PESTE

"Right," breathed Frank. He replaced the Polaroids, rewound the tape, and began to play it one last time. As the video leader ran he swung around to face his computer and typed in a series of commands, then pressed the final key. The words SENDING VIDEO TRANSMISSION appeared next to the blinking cursor. He typed in another line—SENDING GIF OF CRIME SCENE PHOTOS—rose and took the stack of Polaroids to his scanner. Its light flashed blindingly as it made digital copies of the photos. Frank watched it, brooding, as he

waited for the transmissions to go through.
When he reached the pictures of the coffin
lid, sliding each beneath the scanner's flap,
he frowned.

Something there. There was something
there . . .

He reached for the newspaper he'd
brought down with him and unfolded it,
fighting off a rush of excitement as he read
the front page.

POLICE MOVE TO CLEAN UP
CRUISING IN PARK

Beside the headline was a photo of the
spot where last night's murder victim had last
been reported seen by several anonymous
eyewitnesses. The picture showed the wooded
area at the base of the bridge. In the corner of
the frame, the bridge's concrete abutment
reared. Written across it in acid yellow spray
paint was a single word.

PESTE

He knew of Volunteer Park, of course; it had been a notorious gay cruising spot since the early 1970s. But he had never been there at night, certainly had never driven down this rutted spur of an access road, gravel and broken glass crunching beneath the Cherokee's tires. The place looked ruinous, mist threading between sickly looking trees, strands of moss hanging from the bigger firs and broken bottles and squashed beer cans everywhere. Looming above it all the monolithic shadow of the bridge hung like something from a nightmare, a vast dark punitive presence. Beneath it the woods sprawled, a desolate nightscape.

But the woods were not empty. Far from it. A line of cars snaked along the narrow road, and more cars were parked alongside, making the passage even more precarious. Frank eased the Cherokee between vehicles crawling almost at a standstill, their passengers staring out the windows at him with measuring eyes. He finally found a spot to pull over. Zipping up his jacket, he slung his hands into his pockets and got out.

Vapor from his breath flowed uneasily into the cold mist rising from the ground. From overhead echoed the steady drone of traffic on the bridge. He could hear voices nearby, men talking and calling to each other in hushed tones, the occasional burst of raucous laughter. Gingerly he stepped over a guardrail and headed into the woods, wandering for several minutes until he found a bicycle path, now heavily trafficked by men and boys, solitary or in pairs, now and then a group of three or four. As they approached Frank on the path their eyes would rake over him appraisingly, taking in the tall rangy figure, his thick hair stirred by the breeze. But when they caught his expression, at once detached and consumed by something very much like rage, they quickly looked away, or left the path for the anonymous shelter of the trees.

After several minutes he found what he was looking for: a broad footworn trail that led up a steep embankment toward the bridge. He half walked, half ran up the slope, ignoring the curious and sometimes hostile looks he got from men accustomed to their own modes of conduct here. Young men milled in front of the concrete abutments. Solitary figures leaned suggestively against the wall, waiting to be approached, waiting for the right shadow to emerge from the surrounding darkness. There was the flare of matches and cigarette lighters, the glint of bluish light from a bottle. Marijuana smoke mingled with the scent of expensive cologne and a faint underlying odor of sweat and heated flesh.

Frank fought the urge to shout "Fire!" grab a boy so young he was yawning at the late hour and yell at him: *Are you nuts?* But the habits of desire die hard, even in the shadow of a brutal killing.

Especially in the shadow of a killing, thought Frank, and he shuddered, recalling what he had said to Catherine scant hours ago: *Everyone pretends. We all make believe.* He glanced up, and, for a second, his eyes met those of the young boy, hesitating a few feet away to see if Frank was acknowledging him. Frank gazed at him sadly and shook his head. The boy turned away, his face completely blank. *Make believe. Act like nothing's wrong,* Frank thought bitterly, and continued up the hill.

The sounds of traffic grew louder, and in counterpoint to this so did the sound of voices. Two well-dressed men in business suits and expensive trench coats laughed loudly at some private joke, glancing aside at Frank with guileless faces; and this time it was Frank who looked away. His feet slid on loose scree, and he almost lost his balance. But finally he stood at the top of the rise. He paused, catching his breath, then raised his head and saw what he had come to find—the acid yellow graffiti painted high above the heads of all those shadowy figures.

PESTE

He stood and stared up at for several minutes, brooding. *Peste* meant "plague" in French, another stray bit of knowledge he recalled from school. *Pestilence.* And of course who would notice it, just another bit of scribbled nonsense, like BAT 47 or SAMO or BLEDSOE RULES. Anyone who *did* take note would make the obvious connection: more banal homophobic bullshit from some religious zealot, shouting "fag" with a French accent.

Only it seemed as though this particular zealot had a deadly mission. Frank narrowed his eyes, gazing at the solitary word until it began to swim. He blinked and looked away, fighting sudden dizziness.

All around him are corpses. Walking stiffly through the drowned wasteland, stumbling toward him with arms outstretched and at the last instant shrinking back into the shadows when he does not move to embrace them. Behind their tortured figures the trees writhe and scrape barren branches against the sky. Tendrils of smoke rise from them, and from the ground. Frank's shoulders tense, he grimaces as his nostrils fill with the odor of sewage and rotting flesh. His tongue tastes of cold cinders and something else, the thick coppery tang of blood. He digs his hands deeper into his pockets, staring now with trancelike intensity into the darkness. Two men approach him on the trail, their motions jerky, almost hesitant. It is only when they are within several feet of him that Frank sees the skeins of flesh unraveling from their faces, the exposed bones of their hands and wrists protruding through skin burned black as charred paper. He sucks his breath in and takes a step backward; but they cannot see him, they pass him slowly, almost dreamily, their ruined faces turned toward him so he can see where their eyes have been stitched shut with catgut, and their lips, the flesh torn at the corners of their mouths. They stagger past him and he gasps softly.

Something pulses inside him, desire and rage and loathing, a blazing horror that finds its reflection in the cadavers lurching through the blasted forest. He struggles to control his breathing, to slow his pounding heart, then turns to watch as the two spectral forms melt into the night.

And then Frank saw him. A lone figure walking very slowly down the path, his shoulders hunched. He wore jeans, a dark nondescript baseball jacket, dark baseball cap pulled tight onto his forehead. From beneath its brim Frank glimpsed small, deepset eyes glancing around furtively, watching the couples as they made their way through the woods. The ragged whispers he heard moments before cohere into distinct words—

The blood-dimmed tide is loosed—

And once again Frank saw the skeleton burning in the forest, its screams ripping through the trees as a figure lurked in the shadows, watching. A figure in jeans and dark jacket, a baseball cap hiding his features.

The Frenchman.

Frank stared at him, mouth parted. But before he could say anything, before he could move, the other man lifted his head. And saw Frank standing there, watching him.

And, somehow, recognized him: as Frank had recognized the killer. For an instant their eyes held, the thread between them drawn taut. Which broke without warning, when abruptly the Frenchman spun and fled.

Frank lunged after him. Past trees and through brush, branches slashing his face and his feet stumbling on stones and broken bottles. His breath came in sharp bursts as he sprinted, leaving the path and following the other man uphill toward the bridge. Ahead of him came outraged cries as the Frenchman knocked someone aside, more shouts and curses as others scrambled to get out of his way. Frank panted, stooping as he dodged though dense foliage, not noticing where thorns tore at his sleeves and blood welled from his hand. The Frenchman seemed to know hidden trails here, zigzagging up the hillside and disappearing for a minute at a time, before Frank spotted him again, clambering up the slope. The Frenchman leaped across a small footbridge, knocking over a slightly built man and for a moment stumbling. Frank put on a burst of speed, but already the other man was up and running once more.

Now he was beneath the bridge. Men watched him, stunned, from where they stood beside the abutment; others hastily retreated into the woods. Frank caught a glimpse of the Frenchman's back, crashing through an overgrown thicket just past the last massive concrete pier. Frank took off after him, shoving his way through the brush until he found himself at the bottom of yet another incline, this one leading up to the road.

The Frenchman was nowhere in sight. Frank stopped, looking around frantically but seeing nothing. Seconds later something dark pulsed at the corner of his vision: he looked up sharply, to see the Frenchman on the bridge above him. With a gasp Frank took off running again, pulling himself up the hill by grabbing onto bushes and broken saplings.

Then he was at the top, climbing over the bridge railing until he stood on the sidewalk.

Momentarily blinded by the glare of street-lights, headlights, deafened by the roar of nighttime traffic. He blinked, shading his eyes, and saw him—running against traffic on the narrow walkway. Frank wheeled and raced after him.

As he did so the Frenchman looked back. At sight of Frank his face contorted, and, without looking, he darted into the oncoming traffic. Horns blared, tires squealed as cars swung to avoid hitting him. Frank slowed his running, looking for a gap in the traffic, then jumped into the street in pursuit.

In the far lane the Frenchman raced between cars, and Frank followed him. In their wake the bridge became a howling chaos of horns and shouts, cars swerving everywhere, the convulsive shock of metal hitting metal, broken glass sparking the air. A pickup truck spun out of control into the opposite lane, barreling toward Frank. With a cry he threw himself onto the road, rolling, as the truck screeched to a halt inches from his face. Before the driver could register his shock Frank was gone, stumbling to his feet and racing down the center lane. Here he regained his full stride, chasing the Frenchman like a defensive back after a breakaway runner.

But the Frenchman had found the center

lane as well. He put distance on Frank, springing now toward the apex of the bridge. For an instant Frank saw him, darting into the flow of traffic again. There were more horns blaring, more curses. And the Frenchman disappeared from sight.

Cars skidded, slamming into each other in a chain reaction that reached all the way to where Frank ran, finding a path through the stopped vehicles. He sprinted onto the opposite sidewalk, stopped, and spun around, looking in vain for the Frenchman.

He was gone.

Frank stood there for a moment, hands clenching and unclenching; then drifted back into the herd of stalled cars. He searched through them intently, striving to find any sign of the fleeing man.

Nothing. Then from farther down the bridge a man threw his car door open and jumped out.

"He jumped!" he shouted urgently. "I saw him!"

Frank ran to the man. "Where?"

The driver pointed at the bridge railing. "Over the side."

Frank turned and ran to the edge of the bridge. He grabbed the rail with his hands and stared over it, down into smoothly moving black water, its dark surface broken here and there by small whitecaps stirred by the night wind.

A long jump. Not suicidal, but dangerous enough to stop any sane man from leaping, unless he had a good reason.

The Frenchman had a good reason. Frank shook his head, staring futilely at the river below. He saw no sign of any motion in the water, save its normal flow downstream: no frantic swimmer, no body bobbing in the darkness.

How could he have escaped?

Frank stood there for several more minutes, scanning the restless water. At last he turned away, his face contorted with suppressed fury and frustration, and slowly began the long walk back across the bridge, through the angrily milling crowd of drivers and passengers and wrecked vehicles, past the first wailing police cars rushing to the scene. He kept walking until he reached the guardrail, and wearily swung himself over it, and began the long trek through the woods and back to his own car.

And so, of course, he could not have seen the dark figure hanging by outstretched arms from one of the struts beneath the bridge; holding on to the metalwork beneath the walkway, a seam of blood spilling down one arm from a wound in his hand as the Frenchman twisted his head to watch in the distance another solitary figure, head bent as it trudged down the embankment, away from the bridge.

MILLENNIUM
CHAPTER
14

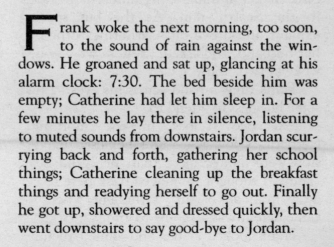

F rank woke the next morning, too soon, to the sound of rain against the windows. He groaned and sat up, glancing at his alarm clock: 7:30. The bed beside him was empty; Catherine had let him sleep in. For a few minutes he lay there in silence, listening to muted sounds from downstairs. Jordan scurrying back and forth, gathering her school things; Catherine cleaning up the breakfast things and readying herself to go out. Finally he got up, showered and dressed quickly, then went downstairs to say good-bye to Jordan.

She sat at the kitchen table, kicking idly at the rungs of her chair and nibbling at a piece of toast. "Hi, Daddy," she said thickly.

He leaned down to kiss her. "Sounds like you got the sniffles."

"Uh-huh." Jordan nodded.

"The principal at her new school says there's something going around—a bunch of kids were out yesterday," Catherine elaborated. "Finish your orange juice, honey. We don't want to be late to school your first week . . ."

He and Catherine stood in the front doorway, watching as their daughter walked out to meet the school bus, her bubble-gum pink slicker and matching umbrella beacons in the Seattle rain. As the bus spewed exhaust and drove off, Catherine turned to her husband, and asked, "Where were you? I woke at two, and you were gone."

Frank drew a hand across his eyes. "I had some business to attend to."

"At two o'clock in the morning?" Catherine's low voice and bemused expression were almost more than he could bear. "Frank, I thought we moved back here to get away from all of this. I thought when we came here it was all going to end."

Frank looked at her and smiled ruefully.

He reached to lay his hand alongside her cheek, then leaned forward to kiss her. "I know," he said. "It will end. I promise. It will."

But as he watched her drive off, he thought, *It never ends, really. No matter where you go, no matter how far: it never, ever ends.*

Two hours later he was in Bob Bletcher's office. Bletcher stood at the back of the room, staring at the spare man poised in front of a blackboard covered with bizarre phrases: snippets of poetry, random words pulled from the videotape Frank Black had brought him. Around the lieutenant stood more than a dozen of his detective force and associated personnel. He'd called them in for this briefing after Frank rang him in the middle of the night, telling him about the man he'd pursued across the bridge and exhorting the detective to allow Frank to make a presentation based on what he'd discovered. Bletcher had agreed, reluctantly. That morning he'd rounded up his staff, short-circuiting more than one coffee break and interrupting several detectives who'd already been working round the clock on this case.

Now Bletcher's reluctance grew even more deep. Not so much because he doubted Frank—he'd *seen* Frank perform some of the feats of investigative legerdemain that had made him a legend—but because he didn't. Bletcher *wanted* to believe Frank Black; and on some, perhaps unconscious, level the detective knew that he *did* believe him. There was something about Frank, the way that your attention focused on him, even while not totally buying what he was saying: the way his gaunt face caught the light and held it. Even in a roomful of people, you would always notice him first, the quiet, loose-limbed man with the haunted eyes, standing off to the side and watching, watching. It was almost as though he had a greater density of being than other people; as though, compared to him, the rest of them were merely shadows.

A snort of disgust brought Bletcher's attention back to earth. He glanced aside, saw two of his detectives staring disdainfully at the front of the room. Bletcher looked back to see Frank pointing his remote at the VCR Bletcher had set up, alongside a TV monitor and blackboard and small table scattered with Frank's notes.

"This is him," Frank was saying, his voice low but still commanding. He leaned over to

adjust the contrast on the TV. The screen
showed an enlarged, extremely grainy image,
a digital array of gray and black pixels that
formed a sort of impressionistic vision of a
man's face. A dull, piggish-looking face,
coarse-featured, his skin even in this imper-
fect transmission clearly showing gouges left
by acne scars. His thin lips moved slowly,
forming words; but then Frank paused the
image. He had not yet switched on the audio.
He glanced out at his audience, bellicose
detectives with crossed arms and dubious
expressions, a few faces more openly inter-
ested. But they were all listening. Bletcher
watched as Frank took a deep breath, and felt
a stab of sympathy for him.

Okay, Frank, he thought. *Here's your
chance. Do your damnedest.*

"The dancers called him 'the Frenchman,' "
Frank began, indicating the frozen image on
the monitor, "because he held poems to the
window. Poems written in French. I was able to
have the picture and audio enhanced off the
original—"

He moved away from the monitor, at
the same time taking aim with the remote.
The frozen video image jumped back to life.
The Frenchman's voice filled the room. It,
too, had been enhanced, a hollow robotic

tone that barely sounded human at all; but the words were clear.

"*I want to see you dance on the blood-dimmed tide . . .*"

As he spoke, Frank copied his words onto the chalkboard—

I WANT TO SEE YOU DANCE ON
THE BLOOD-DIMMED TIDE—WHERE
THE CEREMONY OF INNOCENCE IS
DROWNED.

He put down his chalk, picked up the remote, and once more paused the tape. When he looked up, fifteen bemused faces stared back at him.

Bletcher folded his arms. "What does it mean?" he asked, his voice authoritative but not hostile.

Frank nodded, acknowledging him. "It's from a poem called 'The Second Coming,' by William Butler Yeats." One or two people made appreciative sounds, recognizing the title. Frank went on and recited, " '*Things fall apart, the center cannot hold. Mere anarchy is loosed upon the world. The blood-dimmed tide is loosed and everywhere the ceremony of inno-cence is drowned.*' "

He paused, just long enough for everyone

to register his words, and said, "He's writing about the apocalypse." Then he started the tape again, turning back to the chalkboard and transcribing the Frenchman's twisted litany.

"*This is the second death—the abominable and the fornicators—this is the second death—you'll have your part in the lake—*"

Bletch shifted, surreptitiously looking around to see how the others were taking this. Their faces were rapt if skeptical.

At least he got their attention, thought Bletcher.

In his seat, Giebelhouse fidgeted, frowning. "The second death?" he demanded. "What the hell is that?"

Next to him Detective Kamm cocked his head. "It's from the Bible," he said. His tone and expression told Bletcher that Kamm, at least, didn't think this was so crazy.

"*—the great plague in the maritime city,*" the Frenchman intoned in his infernal whisper. "*You'll have your part in the lake which burns with fire and brimstone.*"

Frank stepped in front of the screen as the tape began to loop once more.

"That line is from Revelation. '*Death and hell were cast into the lake of fire. The abominable and the fornicators. This is the second death.*'"

Bletcher nodded almost imperceptibly. In the room around him all eyes were on Frank Black.

"So what's he trying to say?" broke in Giebelhouse belligerently.

"He's preaching," offered Bletcher.

"He's prophesying," countered Frank.

Giebelhouse lifted his chin, his tone combative. "The end of the world?"

Frank pointed to the last two lines on the blackboard. *"The great plague in the maritime city."* He paused to let this sink in, then translated, " *'La grande peste de la cité maritime.'* 'Peste' was the word written on the lid of the buried coffin."

The detectives stared at him uncomprehending. Some of them shook their heads. A few muttered in outright disbelief.

"It's from Nostradamus," Frank explained. "The sixteenth-century apocalyptic poet. He wrote hundreds of quatrains—four-line poems which foretell the end of all things."

Giebelhouse nodded, his expression mock conviction. "Like rap music."

A few people laughed nervously, but most continued to stare at Frank with tense, barely restrained hostility. Bletcher uncrossed his arms and put on his best Good Cop expression.

"So you think the killer's fulfilling the prophecy?" he asked, feeding Frank lines.

Frank gave the detective a quick look that might have been gratitude, then nodded. "*The great plague in the maritime city will not stop until death is avenged,*" he recited. "*By the blood of a just man, taken and condemned for no crime. The great lady is outraged by the pretense.*"

He stopped, gazing out at the rest, waiting to see if any of them would respond; to see if anyone got it.

No one did.

"Seattle," he went on, trying to keep his voice even. "The maritime city. AIDS, the great plague. Death avenged by a just man, taken and condemned for no crime."

In his seat, Kamm nodded excitedly. "The killer thinks he's righteous. A just man."

Frank's eyes glittered. "Yes."

Bletcher tipped his head back, switching from Good Cop to Devil's Advocate. "So who's the great lady, and why is she outraged?"

Frank gave him the slightest hint of a smile: *touché*. "The killer is in conflict about his sexuality. He feels guilt, quite possibly from his mother. *She* is the 'great lady.' So, in an effort to feel 'normal,' he goes to peep shows, to try to feel something toward women—desire, love, anything. But all he feels is anger . . . Anger that fuels a psychosis which distorts and twists his view of reality."

Giebelhouse snorted. "Twists it to fit some screwy French poetry?"

Frank stared at him impassively. "The killer doesn't see the world like everyone else."

A long moment of silence. Then Bletcher's voice rang out, his tone challenging. "How *does* he see it?"

For an instant the detective's eyes locked with Frank's, defying him to tell the truth, to reveal what it was Frank Black saw.

At the front of the room Frank met the other man's gaze. When he replied it as with a single word:

"Differently," he said, and turned back to the VCR.

"Wait a second," Giebelhouse contested hotly. "You say this guy is angry at women. That he cruises boys, but then he killed this John Doe we found burned in the forest. How does that work? What the hell kind of M.O. is that?"

"He's very confused," said Frank.

Giebelhouse grunted. "Undoubtedly."

"His way of dealing with it is by fulfilling

a prophecy. Avenging the great plague that confuses his own dark desires and justifies his mother's outrage. It's also why he rearranged the position of female victim, to have her arms crossed upon her chest. Out of some twisted respect for her."

Giebelhouse shook his head stubbornly. "I don't buy it."

Beside him Kamm nodded, but reluctantly. "It's a good story," he said, "but I agree. The evidence just doesn't support it."

"The hairs we pulled off the female victim were from a black male," chimed in Bletcher.

For the first time Frank's voice rose. "There has only been one incident of a black male serial killer. Statistically it's improbable."

"So we just throw out the evidence," Giebelhouse began angrily, but Frank cut him off.

"Those hairs could have been planted or picked up before the murder. They could have been left in the body bag. I've seen that before."

Giebelhouse shot him an impatient glance, then turned to Bletcher. "Look, Bob. We're not the FBI. We've got limited resources. We go chasing the wrong guy, we could end up with more victims. I don't think we have the time to waste. Do you?"

Bletcher stood there, silent, taking it all in. The looks of consternation and annoyance and just plain boredom on the faces of his staff, the grainy nightmarish video image intoning its dreadful liturgy of blood and redemption. And in front of them all the embattled figure of Frank Black, his expression open but uncompromising, the VCR remote in his hand like a blade. The detective waited, not wanting to admit that his heart was clenching inside him, not wanting to admit that he was waiting for Frank to come to his own defense, to offer something besides the doomsday ramblings of a madman as an explanation for a murder.

But Frank said nothing. Only stood there, preternaturally calm as he surveyed the expectant faces of the detectives turning from Giebelhouse to himself to Bletcher, and then gazed into Bletcher's eyes as well.

The chief detective waited another moment. Then, "No," he said. The word held all the weight of his eighteen years on the force. "No. I'm sorry, Frank."

A strained silence filled the room. A line had been drawn: Bletcher and Giebelhouse and the others were on one side; an interloper on the other. Without a word Frank turned and hit the eject button on the VCR. He took the videotape and handed it to Bletcher.

"I've got to get home to my family," he said. And left.

He found the Cherokee in the parking garage beneath Social Services, slid inside, and pulled the door shut after him. There, alone in the artificial half-light beneath several thousand tons of steel and concrete, he allowed himself a moment to let go—just an instant, a second of clarity when he was neither Catherine's husband nor Jordan's father nor a bright white template upon which Evil could write its name, over and over and over again until he collapsed—a moment in which he was nothing but Frank Black, a small spark of consciousness with neither conscience nor knowledge to tether him to this city, this world.

And a moment was all it lasted. Because the world *was* there, pressing its face against the window, demanding his attention. Catherine was right: it wouldn't go away, and no amount of pretending would ever change that. At the thought of Catherine the nausea and defeat lodged in his chest began to melt away; and then Catherine brought images of Jordan, her eyes squinched shut as she shrieked with delight, her face snuggling up between her parents in bed on a Sunday morning. And for a moment, seeing them both there, the two people who were more precious to him than anything on earth—for that moment, Frank was content not to pretend at all.

A car whooshed past, the sound magnified by the cavernous space of the parking garage. Frank started, blinking as he cleared his head of everything that had crowded it: Jordan, Catherine, Bletcher, the Frenchman. He reached for the ignition and started the car, and began to pull out of the lot.

He was halfway down the exit ramp, squinting into the unaccustomed brightness of gray daylight filling the arch that led outside, when suddenly a hulking figure darted in front of the Cherokee. Frank slammed on the brakes, the tires squealing as the car heaved to a stop. The figure pounded on the front hood angrily, then moved toward the driver's door. Frank's mouth tightened when he saw that it was Bletcher.

He rolled the window down. Rain gusted in through the opening, soaking Bletcher's suit jacket; but the detective paid it no mind.

"Tell me why I'm wrong!" he cried. His hands tightened on the edge of Frank's window. "Why should I listen to you?"

Frank shook his head, trying to keep his voice even, trying not to sound judgmental. "You're in a hard position, Bob. You've got people to answer to, a department to run—"

"Tell me how you know—how *you're so sure!*" Bletcher's urgent tone grew almost beseeching. "How do you do it, Frank?"

Frank said nothing. After a moment Bletcher raised his head. "You see it or something," he prodded.

Frank sighed. "It's complicated, Bletch."

"You see it, don't you!"

Frank said nothing. Rain slanted through the garage opening, rattling across the windshield. At last he said, "I see what the killer sees."

"What?" Bletcher dipped his head so it poked through the driver's window. "Like a— a psychic?"

"No." Frank spoke slowly, deliberately; as though he were explaining some intricate mechanism to his daughter. "I put myself in his head. I become the thing we fear most."

"How?"

"I become capability. I become horror." Frank's words dropped like stones heaved from a cliff. "What we know we become in our heart of darkness. It's my gift . . . it's my curse. And it's why I retired," he finished, looking up for the first time into Bletcher's intense, almost frightened eyes.

"Then what the hell are you doing here, Frank?" the detective whispered. "Get out. Leave it alone."

Frank's expression sloped into exhaustion. "I tried."

"What brought you back?" demanded Bletcher.

But Frank only shook his head. "Some other time, Bletch," he said softly, rolling up the window. And as the detective stared somberly after him, he pulled away and drove off into the rain.

Catherine's car wasn't in the driveway when he got home. Frank glanced at his watch— after three, Jordan would already be back from school. He parked and sprinted through the rain onto the porch. And stopped.

The front door was open. No sounds came from inside: no after-school chatter from Jordan, answering Catherine's gentle questions; no radio; no cheerful theme music from Wishbone or any other of his daughter's favorite shows. He pushed the door gently and stepped into the front hall.

"Catherine?"

No answer. The boxes Catherine was going to take to the recycling center had not been moved. The newspaper was where he'd left it that morning, unread, still bound in plastic. "Catherine?" he called again, heading for the kitchen. "Jordan?"

The kitchen was empty. There was no note on the counter. The LCD readout on the answering machine read "0." In the middle of the floor a magazine lay where it had fallen, spine up.

"*Catherine!*" Frank shouted, and raced to the second floor.

In Jordan's room the bed had been made, with its new pink spread and new stuffed bulldog keeping guard by his daughter's pillow. He turned away and started for the other bedroom, pausing to glance in the bathroom. The waste-basket had been overturned, spilling tissues across the floor. On the side of the white porcelain tub, the crimson imprint of a child's hand glowed like a warning beacon.

"Jordan," breathed Frank. He fled the room, his footsteps echoing through the house as he ran downstairs and back outside.

He was halfway across the lawn, heart pounding as rain lashed his face, when he heard a door slam.

"Frank! Wait, Frank!" Shielding his eyes against the rain, Frank turned to see his neighbor, Jack Meredith, running from his house. "Frank—"

"Have you seen Catherine and my daughter?" Frank shouted.

Meredith nodded excitedly, his round face red with exertion. He was panting, half-in and half-out of his raincoat, and tugged ineffectually at the hood as he spoke. "I was just coming to leave you a note," he said breathlessly. "She couldn't reach you, and I—"

"Where are they?"

"They went to the hospital—"

"What happened?"

Meredith shook his head, trying to catch his breath. "Your little girl—she had some kind of seizure . . ."

His words died away. Jack Meredith stood alone in the rain, watching as Frank leaped back into his car. Moments later the Cherokee peeled out of the driveway. The older man raised his hand in mute farewell, then turned and trudged back to his own home.

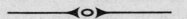

Over the years, Frank had spent too many hours in hospitals. The only time he cared to recall was the night of Jordan's birth, nearly seven years ago.

As he hurried through the Emergency Room entrance, that day came back to him: the same faintly reassuring smells of disinfectant and air-conditioning, the same crisp undercurrent of P.A. announcements, beepers, telephones, murmuring voices.

Now it all seemed utterly sinister. The doctors standing in the hallway, conferring in hushed tones; the cabal of ER nurses behind their station; green-clad technicians hurrying in and out of the elevators. Frank stood helplessly in the middle of the corridor, looking for someone to ask for directions. That was when he saw two orderlies shoving a gurney down the hall. A small form lay on it, sheet pulled up to its chin. An O_2 mask covered the child's face, so he couldn't discern if it was Jordan or not. Trailing the gurney was a doctor, rapidly scanning a clipboard. There were traces of blood on the medics' gowns, and on the sheet covering the child's body.

"Jordan," whispered Frank. He started blindly after the gurney, nearly bumping into a nurse. Immediately he accosted her.

"My daughter was brought in here— Jordan Black—"

The nurse frowned. "Jordan Black?" She glanced down at a sheaf of papers in her hand, but before she could say anything Frank heard another voice.

"Frank—"

"Catherine!" He hurried to where she stood, exhausted, alongside the elevator entrance, and desperately grabbed her arms. "What happened to her?"

Catherine shook her head, fighting tears. Her voice was thick. "I was in the kitchen when I heard this thump upstairs. I found her on the floor in the bathroom. She'd passed out and hit her head on the sink. They're running tests."

"Where is she?"

Catherine gestured limply at the elevator. "In Pediatric ICU. She's sleeping now. They sedated her . . . she's got a very high fever."

When the elevator doors opened he followed her inside, elbowing in among nurses and medics, a woman holding a heart-shaped helium balloon and a teddy bear. They got out at Pediatrics, and he walked numbly alongside his wife. The cheerful yellow walls with their colorful posters and children's drawings seemed monstrous to him, mocking the pale figures he glimpsed inside the rooms they passed. A girl as thin as a wraith, her bald head gleaming beneath the glow of a TV tuned in to *Barney*; a man sitting with head bowed alongside a narrow hospital bed; two small children squabbling with their older brother, tugging at his hospital pajamas.

"Here." Catherine stopped outside a room, its door ajar. "In here . . ."

He entered, Catherine behind him. It took him several moments to find his daughter, surrounded as she was by blinking monitors, the transparent coils of an IV, the unyielding bars of a hospital bed.

But there she was, a tiny figure beneath yellow sheets and a machine-made quilt with tulips on it. Frank blinked and dashed a hand across his eyes, then walked to the bed. Jordan's face was chalk white, her curling hair matted to her head. On her brow a Care Bears bandage covered a nasty-looking bump. The IV snaked into her arm. Her small hand protruded from beneath the quilt, palm open. Frank bent over and rested his own palm upon her forehead.

"They're pretty sure it's just a very bad flu reaction," Catherine said softly. "The doctor says it's not uncommon for children with very high fevers to have these seizures with them."

Frank shook his head, his throat tight. "When will we know?"

"They're calling in a specialist."

"Why isn't he here yet?"

Catherine sighed. "She's on her way."

Frank lowered his head to brush his lips across his daughter's cheek. "So fragile," he breathed.

He stayed like that for several minutes, watching the slow rise and fall of Jordan's chest beneath the blankets, listening to the steady percolating of the IV. At last he looked over at Catherine.

"You should try to rest," he said. He inclined his head at a cot alongside one wall, neatly made with clinical white sheets and pillow. "I'll stay here."

"We'll both stay here," Catherine replied, and she pulled a chair alongside him to continue her vigil.

It was late when he woke, sprawled in the chair where he had finally fallen asleep. Someone had dimmed the lights in the room, and even from where he sat he could hear how hushed the Pediatric Unit had become. Catherine lay passed out atop the cot; she hadn't even bothered to get under the covers. In her hospital bed Jordan lay just as she had earlier, her position unchanged save that her mouth was very slightly parted, and her hand had curled into a fist. Frank remained motionless in his chair and watched her for a long time.

He must have dozed off again: a sound woke him, and he opened his eyes to see the night nurse entering the room, her tread soft but brisk. She carried a pannier of medical supplies. Frank watched her, unmoving, as she stepped to Jordan's bed and set down the pannier, removed the apparatus for drawing blood. Taking Jordan's limp arm she swabbed it, then withdrew a needle connected to the slender tubing that led to a hemo vial. In her bed Jordan stirred, and the nurse murmured to her gently. A few seconds later the transparent tubing darkened to crimson, as blood filled it and the waiting vial.

The nurse glanced over her shoulder at him, then back at Jordan. He continued to stare wide-eyed at the needle in her hand.

"Frank?" Catherine's low voice came to him from across the room. She blinked sleepily, shot a quick concerned look at Jordan to make sure the girl was okay. Then she gazed curiously at her husband again. "What is it, Frank?"

His eyes narrowed, his expression grew more intent, almost hungry. "He's taking blood." Warmth stabbed behind his eyes; he felt a searing heat surge up his spine.

Catherine shook her head, confused. "Who?"

"The killer." He got to his feet, meeting her stare and nodding. "He's got more bodies. He's buried them alive."

Catherine hesitated. Looking quickly at their daughter on the hospital bed, then back at her husband. "Go, Frank," she said. Her voice was urgent.

Silently he grabbed his coat and rushed from the room.

B letcher and his men were already in the forest when Frank arrived. He saw the line of police and undercover cars parked alongside the desolate stretch of road and heard the distant baying of bloodhounds. He sprinted through the undergrowth, not slowing until the first pinpricks of light began to show through the thicket of trees, dozens of flashlights bobbing through the darkness. The wind blew cold up from the river, and with it the smell of stone and snowmelt. Overhead the moon broke through the clouds, its uneasy glow touching branches and mounded leaves with silver before it disappeared once more behind the clouds. As Frank drew nearer to the search party the metallic chatter of radios and walkie-talkies destroyed the last illusion of silent woodland.

He found Bletcher, trailing the rest of the group. Like the others he was heavily bundled against the cold, his breath misting the air. He raised his head in greeting when he saw Frank, then lifted the hand holding his walkie-talkie as it blatted loudly.

"... *we've covered the area a mile north down to the river. Nothing.*"

Bletcher frowned. "Copy." He slowed his steps to let Frank catch up with him, shuffling through frost-rimed leaves. "I'm going to call this off, Frank. Local search-and-rescue's been here for nearly an hour, and my men have been out for almost that long. This is getting us nowhere. We'll come back in the light of day."

He stopped, waiting for Frank's reaction, but Frank kept on walking. His head swung back and forth, his hands trailed along the trunks of trees and traced the edges of boulders. "They could be dead by then," he said simply, and forged ahead.

As Bletcher stared after him, Giebelhouse

and Kamm drew up alongside of the chief detective. Giebelhouse gaped at Frank in open disbelief. "Jesus Christ, what's he think?" he sputtered, teeth chattering. "They're cryogenically preserved?"

"What's he doing?" wondered Kamm.

Bletcher shook his head in dismay. "I have no idea." He began to run, following where Frank had turned down a deer trail leading to the river. "But I'm going to find out . . ."

The recent heavy rains had caused the river to flood its banks. Black water extended to the very fringe of the woods, moving swiftly beneath the restless moon. The searchers had stopped here. Their flashlights formed an eerie barrier at river's edge as they wandered back and forth, pointing their beams at the far shore. The dogs whined and pulled at their leashes, sniffing eagerly at the water. Bletcher blinked, shading his eyes as the searchers turned their bright halos on him.

"This is it, Bob," somebody yelled. "We turn back here?"

Bletcher strode toward them, trying to pick out Frank among the milling figures. Sudden splashing stopped him in his tracks; he craned his neck, turning until he saw

Frank Black's lanky form wading into the rushing water.

"Frank!" Bletcher shouted. "What the hell you doing? You'll freeze to death!"

But Frank never paused, just kept on picking his way carefully through the torrent. Bletcher swore angrily, watching as the water rose higher and higher, until it reached Frank's hips.

"Damn it, Frank!"

Bletcher shoved his way through the crowd watching the lone figure in amazement. When he reached the water he stopped. For another minute he watched his friend's spare silhouette wading through the current. Then, taking a deep breath, he stepped into the river.

"Jesus!" The cold bit into him, so intense that for an instant he couldn't move. Before he could think better of it he began to wade across the river. Behind him the other detectives and rescue squad held back, exclaiming loudly.

"You nuts, Bletch?"

"Let him go!"

"For chrissakes, Bob!"

Bletcher ignored them. He forged on, gasping as the water lapped about his ankles, then his calves and thighs, and finally reached his crotch. "Good thing I already have a family," he wheezed as he finally made it to shore.

Ahead of him Frank's flashlight shone through the trees, darting from one copse to another. "Frank! Wait up!" Bletcher shouted, staggering from the water and training his own light on the woods in front of him. He started to run, as much to get the blood flowing in his legs again as for any other reason, nearly stumbling on the slickly frozen ground. When he reached the trees the footing was better, scattered stones and dead leaves that crunched beneath his feet. He tried to keep Frank in sight, the other man's flashlight bobbing through the shadows like a will-o'-the-wisp.

"Frank!" he yelled again, when suddenly his foot struck something hard. There was a dull, hollow *thunk*. Bletcher stopped dead in his tracks and stared at the ground. He raised his foot and brought his heel down hard against the forest floor.

Thunk.

There was something hollow beneath him.

"Frank!" he shouted, his voice rising almost to a scream as he dropped to his knees. "Frank, over here! I found something—"

Frantically he scooped away the leaves. Behind him Frank ran up breathlessly and knelt beside him, the two of them sweeping their hands back and forth as leaves flew up all around them. Within moments the space was cleared. Bletcher gazed down at it, stunned.

"Oh, Christ."

Where the leaves had been was the wooden lid of another coffin. Several small holes had been bored in its surface: airholes. Crooked letters were scratched into the rough grain.

LA GRANDE DAME

Frank and Bletcher worked furiously. "Find the edges!" Frank yelled. "There—"

He pointed to where one corner of the coffin protruded from the earth. Bletcher grabbed it and began trying to yank it loose. As he did so, muffled pounding sounded from beneath the lid, and frenzied, inhuman cries. Bletcher drew up in horror.

"Oh my God—"

"Find the screws—the other one was screwed shut—" Frank shouted. He pulled a Swiss Army knife from his pocket and jammed it down where Bletcher pointed, spearing the center of a metal screw. As he spun it out the muffled shrieks grew louder and even more frantic. The coffin's lid shuddered as whatever was beneath struggled to free itself.

"Here!" Bletcher cried, grabbing the Swiss Army knife from Frank and loosening another screw. His hands shook so badly the knife fell; Frank snatched it back and finished the job.

Now one edge was free. The shrieks became a sustained howl of pure terror. Frank and Bletcher strained with the coffin lid, trying to find enough leverage to pull it loose. The wood began to splinter, at last gave way as they fell backward, grappling for their flashlights. As they did so a figure lurched from the coffin. The stench of excrement and decaying flesh was so strong Bletcher gagged, then recoiled as he gazed in horror at what was toppling onto the ground beside them—

A young man, so filthy it was impossible to discern what color his skin had been, or even if any flesh remained upon his body. He flailed helplessly in the fallen leaves, still screaming. Though now Bletcher could see why the sound had been muffled: the boy's mouth had been sewn shut, and his eyes.

Even his hands been sewn together, rough stitches binding them at the wrists, the skin frayed and thin as bloodied linen. His eyelids were bleeding: he had somehow managed to get them half-open. His face held the starkest, most primal horror Bletcher had ever seen.

"My God," the detective whispered. The boy thrashed, and Bletcher recoiled. Then, as though awakening from a nightmare, he began to shout hoarsely at the top of his lungs.

"Paramedics! We need paramedics over here! PARAMEDICS!"

From across the river came answering cries, loud splashing as the rescue team began to ford the river. The boy's cries gave way to a sort of ululating sob. Frank took him gently in his arms and began to lift him, pausing so that Bletcher could stumble to his feet and help. Together they carried the quaking, delirious figure away from his tomb. His skin was damp and icy to the touch. Frank stared at the bloody figure, dirt and filth caked to his clothes, then put his arms around him and held him close, trying to warm him with his own body. The boy struggled in his embrace, shuddering with cold and terror. Frank thought of holding Jordan when she'd had the chicken pox, her small body alternately chilled and burning with fever, trembling in the night. He tightened his grip on the young man's shoulders and murmured wordlessly, comfortingly; trying, just for an instant, to impart some sense that the world was shifting back to normal; that all would be well; that the nightmare was over.

But Frank knew, in fact, that it was not. He knew the truth of it was that, for some people, the nightmare never, ever, ends.

He craned his neck, looking to where the first searchlights were coming into view, moving rapidly through the darkness as the paramedics raced toward them. A few feet away Bletcher crouched once more at the edge of the makeshift casket, looking down into it with one hand covering his nose and mouth against the smell. Suddenly he gave a harsh gasp and very gingerly reached inside.

There was something in the far corner: a plastic bag. With shaking fingers Bletcher grasped it and pulled it out. It was heavy, the plastic slick with some viscous substance. As he held it up he swung his flashlight around so that the beam played across it.

Within its cloudy plastic sheath a face stared out at him, its eyes already occluded with decay, matted blond hair shrouding its livid cheeks. Gray flesh clung to the knobs of vertebrae that bulged from the base of its neck. One ear had almost been severed. It dangled like a swollen fruit beside her jaw. Across her forehead a word had been carved like a brand.

MYSTERY

"Calamity," Bletcher whispered. Tears of horror and disgust filled his eyes. He got to his feet, trembling, and turned to Frank. As he did so the first paramedics came running into the clearing, and drew up, shocked, to see the chief detective standing there with his macabre trophy.

"They're here to help you," Frank murmured to the young man still struggling and moaning in his grasp. Gently he handed the boy to the paramedics, then straightened and addressed the remaining men.

"There may be others," he said, indicating the surrounding forest. Murmurs of assent went through Bletcher's army, a bark from one of the anxious bloodhounds. Then the search crew fanned out, and began to hunt in earnest.

MILLENNIUM
CHAPTER

18

CHAPTER

81

---◀◉▶---

It was nearly dawn when Frank and Bletcher returned to headquarters. Grimy light filtered through the windows of Bletcher's office. People darted in and out, dropping off papers, delivering faxes and manila file folders. Frank sat in a swivel chair, his eyes closed, face drawn. Behind his desk Bletcher swung restlessly back and forth in his swivel chair, phone cupped to his ear.

A shadow filled the doorway. Someone crossed quietly to where Frank sat and tapped him on the shoulder. His eyes flew open, and he stared up into Giebelhouse's chastened face.

"Here. Thought you could use this," he said, handing Frank a mug of coffee.

Frank took it. "Thanks."

Giebelhouse nodded, a token apology, and leaned against a table. "They found two more coffins. Both were empty."

Frank eyed him coolly. "They wouldn't have been for long."

Behind them Bletcher hung up the phone and quickly turned to the other two men. "He just gave a description of the suspect. White male, late twenties, wearing a ball cap. They're working up an artist's profile now." He paused, staring purposefully at Giebelhouse, and added, "He took blood from the victim."

Giebelhouse said nothing. He stared at Bletcher, then at Frank, finally nodded at the gaunt man. "I'll put it out on the air," he said, and hurried out.

Bletcher waited until he was gone. Then he turned once more to Frank, eyebrows raised.

"The killer's passing judgment," Frank said. His tone held absolute certainty. "He's probably testing that blood, then carrying out his death sentences on the afflicted."

Bletcher lifted his hands in a futile gesture. "So how're we going to catch him?"

"Stake out the crime scenes. Killers are

prone to revisiting them. Get everyone you can spare out there in those woods. Get his picture out. Check any medical facility that handles blood."

Bletcher nodded. "Right. We've already got word out to the labs."

Frank sighed and got to his feet. His clothes were filthy, stained with dirt and blood, and there were dark circles under his eyes. "I've got to call Catherine."

Bletcher pushed the telephone across his desk toward him. As Frank reached for the receiver he said in a strained voice, "Eighteen years, Frank. I don't think I've ever seen anything as terrifying as what I saw tonight."

Frank met his gaze, Bletcher's eyes wide as though still seeing what he had beheld in the forest. "You ever see your kid lying in bed in an emergency ward?"

Bletcher took a deep breath, finally nodded in agreement. As Frank started punching in a number he rose and started for the door, but stopped before stepping into the corridor.

"It made sense to me out there tonight, Frank. What it does to you. What it did to you. Why you quit . . ."

Frank stopped dialing. He stared across the room at the detective, then slowly replaced the handset in its cradle. He sighed, and ran a hand across his exhausted face.

"The cruelty, the unspeakable crimes—it all becomes numbing, depersonalized. Common." He spoke as though he had the words memorized, as though he had repeated them a hundred times before. "After a while you stop feeling anything."

Bletcher shrugged. "What was it, then?"

Frank sighed and eased himself onto the edge of Bletcher's desk. "I was on a serial case in Minnesota. The killer's name was Ed Cuffle. He would choose a neighborhood, go up to a door—all totally at random. If the door was unlocked, he considered it an invitation to go in and slaughter anybody home. Then he'd take Polaroids of his victims and send them to the police."

He took a deep breath, and went on. "That's how serial killers work—that's why they're *serial* killers. They get a rush from the murder itself, the violation; but then they get another rush from not getting caught. So they do it again, and again. It's an addiction; but it's how we catch them, eventually. Because they can't stop killing, and a lot of the time they can't stop leaving a trail. Toying with the police, like a cat playing with its prey. Getting off on it. The danger, the threat of getting caught. That's why it was so difficult to get Cuffle—the utter randomness of his M.O. There was no logic to it. Like breaking a code devised by a madman. It took us months, but we finally caught the guy. He's doing a triple life sentence."

He finished, stared down at his hands. Bletcher waited to see if there was more. When Frank said nothing, he asked, "And that was it?"

Frank lifted his head. His eyes were burning, haunted. "A year later I reached into my mailbox, picking up my mail. Inside there's an envelope addressed to me. No return. And inside—"

His voice grew strained, as though he could barely pronounce the words. "Inside are Polaroids of Catherine at the supermarket. Catherine at school. And suddenly—suddenly the psychic novocaine wore off. The numbness became paralyzing fear."

Bletcher gazed at his old friend with pity and horror. "Did you ever find who sent it?"

"No. I couldn't even leave the house. Why go to work to protect others if you can't even protect your own family? Jordan— Jordan was a miracle to us. The doctors told us we would never be able to conceive. How could I live with myself, knowing she was at risk?"

"But you beat it, Frank." Bletcher shook his head admiringly. "You *did* beat it. How?"

"I was approached by a group of men and women who helped me understand the nature of my facility." He hesitated. "My gift."

Bletcher nodded, encouraging him to go on. "This Millennium Group?"

"Yes."

"They really believe this stuff, then? Nostradamus and Revelations. . . ? The destruction of the world?"

Frank stared at him. A full minute passed before he replied. "They think we can't just sit back and hope for a happy ending."

He reached for the telephone receiver and picked it up, once again began punching in the hospital number. Bletcher watched him. When nothing else was forthcoming, he turned and left. Frank stared after him, frowning as the phone bleated a busy signal. He pressed the receiver to get another dial tone, but as soon as he did, the phone rang.

"Bob Bletcher's office," Frank said, glancing at the door to see if Bletcher was there.

"Bob?" A man's voice.

"No, he just stepped out.

"The caller made an impatient sound. "Can you give him some information for me? It's urgent—"

Quickly Frank swung around, scrabbling at Bletcher's desk for paper. "Let me get a pen—okay."

"Tell him we think we tracked down those blood samples he's looking for. They were sent to a lab the Seattle PD uses downtown."

In Frank's ears was a faint humming. The voice on the other end of the line seemed to grow faint. He swallowed, his mouth flooded with the taste of bile and copper. "Where were they sent from?" he asked, his voice dry.

"That's just it." The caller's tone wavered between frustration and bewilderment. "They were sent through the same channels as the PD. The same courier service. Intraoffice."

"Intraoffice . . ." Frank stared at the door, his mouth suddenly dry. Without saying good-bye he set the phone back in its cradle and stood. The room round him seemed to swim, chairs and desks and bookshelves taking on the liquid contours of a drowned forest, the rotting piers and alleys of a city being inundated by a tide so immense and fast-moving and inescapable that one could only look on in a sort of awe, a sort of transcendent horror that this was the way the world ended. The smell of sewage filled the room, burning petroleum, scorched hair and flesh.

Dust motes spinning slowly above Bletcher's desk lamp coalesced into the fluid silhouette of a woman writhing seductively behind a glass window, a headless corpse encased in black plastic.

"Bob." His voice rang out harshly through the empty office. He ran out into the hallway, looking fruitlessly back and forth. "*Bob!*"

There was no answer. Heart roaring, he began to race down the hall, until he reached the freight elevator. It was several minutes before it arrived. The heavy doors slid open with excruciating slowness, and he leaped inside, furiously punching buttons until at last the doors closed again. Then the elevator descended with even more agonizing languor. Frank stood with his back pressed against the far wall, watching the lights flicker in the LCD readout—3—2—LOBBY—PARKING LEVEL—until his destination scrolled across the screen in bright red letters.

MORGUE

19

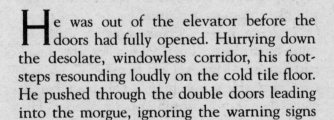

He was out of the elevator before the doors had fully opened. Hurrying down the desolate, windowless corridor, his footsteps resounding loudly on the cold tile floor. He pushed through the double doors leading into the morgue, ignoring the warning signs plastered to doors and wall—

AUTHORIZED PERSONNEL ONLY!
BIOHAZARD ALERT!
PLEASE OBSERVE ALL SAFETY REGULATIONS!

Icily refrigerated air washed over him, sweetness of lactose and formaldehyde, alcohol and disinfectant and the faintest pungent base note of decay. All round him stretched that gruesome archipelago of stainless-steel gurneys, their burden of cadavers and body bags forming ominous peaks where they were shoved anonymously against walls. His feet clattered across a series of drains in the floor, narrow sloping channels leading from the autopsy tables built into the far wall. In front of one of these a white-robed man was bent over a glittering array of scalpels and lenses and briskly efficient-looking surgical knives. Beside him on the table a pallid bloated form lay exposed, its chest cavity opened to reveal ribs like the spars of a ship.

"Excuse me—" Frank drew up next to him, breathless. "I'm looking for the head pathologist—Massey, Curt Massey—"

"Sorry. He's not here." The man barely glanced at Frank, intent on his work. "His desk's over there, you could leave a—"

But Frank did not hear his words. Frank heard other words, a hoarse whisper repeating *I want to see you dance, I want to see you dance* over and over again. He stared at the other man, taking in his gloved hands, his rapt expression as he stooped over the bloodless corpse.

"—message . . ." The man's voice trailed off. He straightened and turned, for the first time looked at Frank standing behind him. In that instant their eyes locked, as they had on the path in Volunteer Park. And behind those eyes Frank saw it all, as exposed as the viscera of the corpse he was dissecting: Tuesday's body in flames; Calamity's torso carefully arranged with arms crossed upon her blood-soaked chest; the dreadful lipless mouth of another corpse, mouth frozen in a rigor of unspeakable horror where the body was imprisoned in its crude coffin.

And Frank saw himself there as well, his own face mirrored in the killer's, his own features as the Frenchman saw them right now, the gaunt avenging angel come to take vengeance upon the bloody prophet.

"No!" The Frenchman shouted. His features contorted with the anguish of being discovered. With one swift motion he grabbed a knife from the table, its blade long and serrated, designed for sawing through bone and muscle. He charged Frank, the knife whistling through the air as he slashed at his throat. Frank dodged, sidestepping behind a body on a gurney. With all his strength he pushed the gurney at the Frenchman, recoiling as the man leaned over the body and the knife swiped dangerously close to Frank's face. Then he shoved at the gurney again, forcing the Frenchman back against the metal counter behind him.

"*Who are you to condemn me?*" the man shrieked, his eyes wild.

"Put that knife down, and we'll talk," Frank responded, trying to keep his voice calm.

But the Frenchman's answer to this was to thrust the knife toward Frank, inches from his cheek. Frank leaned forward, pushing all his weight against the gurney, keeping the Frenchman pinned to the counter. The killer squirmed, trying to escape.

"They're the guilty!" he shouted. "You *know* that!"

Frank shook his head. "Put down the knife."

"I took responsibility," the killer went on, the words coming relentlessly now. "Somebody had to! You see them—"

He gestured crazily with the knife. "—out there where Satan has His throne. The great plague. Somebody has to do it! Nobody ever asks—who takes *responsibility?*"

Frank listened to his ranting, staring at him with piercing eyes as he tried to calculate the madman's next move. The door was far away; all the weapons, all the instruments of the coroner's craft, were on the counter behind the Frenchman. Quickly Frank tried to determine if he could reach one when, without warning, the Frenchman once more lunged at his face. Frank went reeling backward. The Frenchman shoved the gurney, sent it wheeling toward Frank so that it struck him and sent him tumbling to the ground. Above him the gurney began to topple. Vainly Frank tried to spin away, but it was too late: the gurney fell, and with it its grotesque burden, the body falling on top of Frank and pinning him to the floor. He tried frantically to push it off, to escape; but then the Frenchman was there, bending over Frank's face with the knife to Frank's throat.

"This is *prophecy*," he hissed. Only the cadaver was there as any bulwark between the two of them. "The final judgment and victory! This is the way it ends. But you know that . . ."

His mouth twisted into a vicious smile. "You see it, don't you? You see it all—*just like I do*."

Frank stared into his distorted face, and knew that it was true: that the killer saw him. *Recognized* him; recognized his vision, just as Frank had recognized his.

"You know the end is coming!" the French-man cried. "The thousand years is over—"

Suddenly he drove the knife downward at Frank. Gasping, Frank pushed the corpse toward him, so that it caught the blow; then kicked out, trying to slither away on his back.

But the Frenchman was too fast. Tugging the knife free, he scrambled toward Frank, raising the knife to land his last, fatal blow.

"You think you're the one to stop it!" he cried. "You think it can be stopped—"

He drove the blade down, aimed so that it would impale Frank's heart. Frank gasped, struggling futilely to escape, when a thunder-ous explosion tore through the room. Above him the Frenchman's face crumpled into shock as his body was blown backward. Blood spurted from his chest as he slammed against the floor. Frank twisted to see Bob Bletcher standing just inside the double doors leading into the morgue. Vapor sur-rounded the sidearm he kept aimed at the fallen man.

"Frank," he said, making a sideways motion his with head.

Frank got to his knees, looking back at the Frenchman. He was curled into a ball, clutching his chest. Blood soaked his white jacket and latex gloves, oozed from his mouth as he stared at Frank with a strangely intent gaze.

"You can't stop it," he murmured, his voice growing faint. For one last moment his eyes held Frank's. In their icy depths the gaunt man saw imprecation, and warning. "You . . . can't . . . stop . . . it . . ."

Several days later, Catherine stood in the kitchen, hastily finishing her morning coffee. Frank had gone out earlier, pleading an urgent errand and leaving her to deal with Jordan. The girl had been released the day before. They were still waiting for results from the battery of tests she'd been given, but the doctor assured Catherine and Frank that she was out of any immediate danger.

"Children do have seizures sometimes," he'd told them at their last meeting. "And I know that it can be terrifying for a parent to witness one, or its aftermath. But as long as it's associated with something in particular, like a high fever, a seizure of this sort may not be anything to worry about. But we'll wait for the test results, rule out anything that might be worrisome."

So they'd brought her home. And Catherine had gone ahead and arranged for a job interview this morning—an interview she was going to miss if Frank didn't get back soon. She put down her coffee mug and, for the hundredth time, adjusted her skirt, smoothing her hair in its unaccustomed, tidy braid down the back of her linen suit. Then she picked up her earrings where she'd left them on the counter, alongside more copies of her résumé and the job materials the head-hunter had sent her when she was still in D.C.

"Catherine."

She whirled, to see Frank poking his head between the swinging doors that led into the dining room. She smiled.

"I'm glad you're home—I'm going to be late for my interview." She finished putting in her earrings, then glanced back at her husband. Her expression changed from relief to curiosity as he continued to stand there in

the same awkward pose, only his head showing

"Frank? What are you doing?"

He whispered, "Where's Jordan?"

"She's up in her room. What are you
doing, Frank?"

Reassured that the coast was clear, he
pushed the doors open and stepped into the
kitchen. Bundled in his jacket was a tiny
black-and-white ball of fur.

"Oh my God!" Catherine raised her
hands in delight and rushed to him. "Look at
this."

He held the puppy out to her and she
took it in her arms. It squirmed and whimpered, threatening to lick off all her carefully
applied makeup.

"It's a border collie," Frank explained.
"They were all out of basset hounds. Come
on—"

He took the puppy from her and gestured
for her to go upstairs first. She did so, and
Frank followed, whispering *hush* to the wrig-
gling bundle in his arms. At the top of the
stairs he could hear Jordan's excited voice.

"What is it? Tell me, tell me!"

"Close your eyes, honey—c'mon, it's a
special surprise for being such a big brave
girl—"

He waited outside her room, peering in to make sure her eyes were shut. His daughter was still in bed in her pajamas, toy bulldog in her lap, eyes squeezed tight. Beside her, Catherine looked over at him and nodded. He stepped inside.

"I think someone's trying to peek," Catherine scolded.

"What *is* it?" Jordan cried breathlessly. Frank quietly crossed the room to her bed and put the puppy in her lap. Jordan's eyes flew open. She squealed in delight as the puppy lunged at her, eagerly licking her face.

"Oh, Daddy!" She hugged the puppy to her, laughing joyously. "What's its name?"

Frank sat on the bed and smiled. "He doesn't have one yet."

"Can I name him?"

Frank nodded. "He's yours, isn't she?"

The puppy settled into Jordan's arms. His daughter sighed blissfully. "Oh, Daddy. I love him so much."

Catherine reached to take Frank's hand. She gazed at him, her eyes tearing.

"So much for the professional woman's makeup," she said. "I'll be right back—"

So Frank sat there with his daughter, watching her play with the new puppy, sun slanting in through the windows, the smell of fresh coffee percolating through the house. And for a little while he was purely happy, playing make-believe.

"Well," he said at last, his own eyes tearing, "I think I'll let you two get acquainted." He patted Jordan's leg, tousled the puppy's fur, and went into the hall. On his way downstairs he poked his head into the bathroom, where Catherine was putting on fresh lipstick.

"Good luck with the interview."

"Thanks." She turned and gave him a smile almost as blissful as Jordan's. "It really *is* going to be okay, Frank, isn't it? All of this"—she gestured, taking in the room, the little girl in her bedroom with the yapping puppy, the edenic yellow house itself—"all this is just the beginning."

Frank smiled back. "I think you're right," he said, and went downstairs.

At the foot of the steps the morning mail sat on the floor beneath the mail slot in the front door. He paused to pick it up, sorting through junk mail, magazines, flyers, bills forwarded from D.C. Then halting when he came to something else.

It was a letter addressed to him. His name neatly typed on a label, and beneath it their current address.

Frank Black
1910 Ezekiel Drive

The letter had not been forwarded. It had no return address. His heart began to race as he opened it, slid his fingers inside to feel the familiar slick surface of several Polaroids. Before he could remove them Catherine came bounding downstairs.

"I think you've already got a mess to clean up, up there," she announced, cocking a thumb toward the second floor.

"Right," Frank said numbly.

She picked up her purse and briefcase. "Wish me luck," she said, kissing him. Then, noting his tension, "What?"

He looked at her: the sun striking her hair, all the fatigue and worry of the last few days erased. "Nothing," he said. "Be careful. Okay?"

She nodded, smiling, straightened her jacket, and walked outside. Frank watched her go down the sidewalk to her car. As she drove off, he looked down once more at the envelope. With shaking hands he opened it, removed the Polaroids.

They were pictures of Catherine and Jordan. The two of them in the back of the Cherokee, Jordan strapped into her booster seat. Catherine in front of a revolving door, slightly out of focus as she rushed to get inside, out of the rain. A blurry view of Jordan's head.

And, last of all, Catherine and Jordan glimpsed through busy traffic on a city street. The two of them holding hands, waiting for the light to change. Staring at the photo Frank's breath came in ragged bursts; he felt the pressure beginning once more inside his skull as with shaking hands he drew the Polaroid closer to his face.

And saw, behind the fragile images of his wife and daughter caught unawares at a random moment, the distinct outline of a bright yellow car, a logo cheerfully emblazoned on its door:

SEATTLE CITY CAB:
WE'LL ALWAYS FIND YOU,
WHEREVER YOU ARE

ELIZABETH HAND is the author of *Glimmering, Winterlong,* and the World Fantasy Award nominee, *Waking the Moon.* She lives in Maine.

Be sure to look for

MILLENNIUM
GEHENNA

LEWIS GANNETT

BASED ON THE CHARACTERS
CREATED BY
CHRIS CARTER

Coming from HarperPrism

MILLENNIUM
PROLOGUE

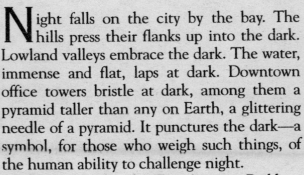

Night falls on the city by the bay. The hills press their flanks up into the dark. Lowland valleys embrace the dark. The water, immense and flat, laps at dark. Downtown office towers bristle at dark, among them a pyramid taller than any on Earth, a glittering needle of a pyramid. It punctures the dark—a symbol, for those who weigh such things, of the human ability to challenge night.

The pyramid is the TransAmerica Building. The city is San Francisco. There, tonight, darkness presents a particular challenge.

Tonight Gehenna will strike.

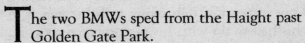

The two BMWs sped from the Haight past Golden Gate Park.

Industrial frat-rock music throbbed in the lead car, the bass lines thundering through the windows, the seats, and the floor, through the five young men with close-cropped hair. Lars drove. Ralph rode shotgun.

In back, squeezed between Dylan and Nick, Eedo wondered where they were going. What they would do. No one had filled him in on the evening's agenda. "Go for a ride, get high," was all Ralph had said. Eedo didn't feel great about the outing. Under his companions' rowdy cheer he sensed a grimness that contradicted the idea of a night on the town. It was making Eedo increasingly uneasy.

He'd known the others about seven months now, ever since he'd abandoned his old existence as the son of simple Chechan immigrants. Ever since he'd made the fateful step of joining the organization that one referred to, with generic vagueness, as the Enterprise. Like any twenty-year-old suddenly sure he'd found his path in life—a path of glory, shared with guys his own age—he'd trusted his new co-workers, seen them as allies, friends.

At first he had. Now Eedo wasn't so sure.

Not at all sure, in fact. He wondered, a knot of tension tightening in his stomach, if this had to do with his performance at work. With its recent slump.

Faith. Discipline. Was he slipping? Was he Enterprise material? Above all, could he work the numbers?

Those questions, their implications, made Eedo afraid.

Streetlights strobed the car's windows. Eedo stared at the road's dipping curves, unwilling to engage eye contact with Dylan on his left, Nick on his right. The rearview mirror occasionally flared the headlights of the BMW following. Like this one, it was new—like this one, full of colleagues. Guys with faith and discipline. Guys who worked the numbers with brutal efficiency.

It's okay, Eedo told himself. It's okay . . .

Lars slowed the car, pulled over to the curb. The other car drew up behind. Eedo looked out at an expanse of dark grass, black stands of trees. They'd stopped at a park. AMBROSE MEMORIAL PARK & GARDENS, Eedo saw on a dimly lit sign by the path that gave entry. Not many people around.

Ralph opened his door, got out, and headed down the path into the park. Eedo watched him merge with foliage, disappear. What now? he wondered.

Nick opened a couple of sweating Coronas and passed one to Dylan. They clinked bottles over Eedo's lap, toasting each other, then took covert swigs. It wouldn't do to get noticed by cops, should any be watching the area. Nick leaned into Eedo's ear.

Eedo steeled himself. He knew what was coming.

"Woof!" Nick exclaimed. "Woof-*woof!*"

"Cut it out," Eedo grumbled. This dog game, the barking, was pushing his buttons. The guys had been going at it since they picked him up. What did it mean?

He didn't want to know, he realized. Nick punched his arm, handed him a Corona. "C'mon," he said teasingly. "Eedo, we're gonna have a blast."

Eedo took a furtive sip, grateful for the beer's calming effect and hoping Nick spoke the truth. He focused on the tune blasting from the car's powerful stereo: "*I wanna get high, so high . . .*"

Eedo wondered: I wanna?

Lars turned to the boys in back. Eedo studied Lars's smooth baby face, the hardness in Lars's eyes that wasn't babylike at all. "The Dark Prince returns," Lars said slyly. Eedo looked up. Ralph, rematerializing from the park's murk, was striding toward them. A small foil-wrapped packet glinted in one of his hands. *Dark Prince*, Eedo thought. That's on target. Ralph recently had been made supervisor of the numbers operation. There was a fellow with faith and discipline—Ralph ran his minions ragged. He leaned through the front passenger-side window, handed Lars the foil packet, and said in a deliberate, oddly deadpan tone, "Tickets to the horror show."

Great, thought Eedo.

Lars unfolded the packet. A slip of paper lay within. Perforated paper—the holes formed a grid of squares that resembled a strip of postage stamps. The squares bore no images, however. They were blank, off-white, slightly smudged.

"*I wanna get high, so high . . .*"

"Yes indeedy," Lars declared, peeling off four squares. He gave them to Ralph, who wheeled away to the second car. Delivering the merchandise, Eedo noted, looking through the rear window. Ralph sauntered back, opened his door, dropped into his seat, and slammed the door hard. Then he retrieved from Lars what remained of the perforated strip.

Lars put the car in gear and shot from the curb.

The car behind followed.

Ralph turned to face Eedo. Slowly, carefully, making sure Eedo had a good view, he tore the paper into its constituent squares.

Acid, Eedo thought, the knot in his stomach twisting tighter. *Blotter LSD, potency unknown, procured from some dealer in a public park.* To Eedo's left, Dylan twitched. To his right, Nick stirred. Eedo wondered if they felt as nervous as he did. If they feared the drug's effect on their mysterious quest, on whatever it was that lay ahead.

Ralph extended a finger to Eedo, the end digit bearing a square.

Eedo looked Ralph in the eyes. They

gleamed with amusement. With something else, too. Maybe pity. Or scorn.

Ralph said, "Fetch the paper, Eedo."

Although he had no choice but to do as he was told, for Ralph's word was law, Eedo hesitated. The finger, the square, came closer. Eedo blinked. Then he took the square, put it in his mouth. And chewed.

It tasted dirty. Bitter.

"*Woof!*" Nick yapped in his right ear.

"*Grrrrr!*" Dylan growled in the left one.

Eedo closed his eyes. He couldn't take the way Ralph was looking at him. The faint smile on his lips. The cold glow in his gaze.

"Good boy, Eedo," Ralph softly. "You're real good, yes you are."

Twenty minutes later Eedo started to feel the burn. The corrosive buzz. His stomach, twistier now than ever, seemed to digest itself. Eat itself up.

They'd driven to a section of the harbor that was inactive even in daytime, still as Stonehenge at night. Piers and warehouses rolled by, dark, gaunt; trash ghosted through the streets, an urban sagebrush of newsprint, food wrappers, ragged plastic bags.

Eedo had become much more aware of the bodies flanking him, of legs and shoulders penning him in. The squeeze, tight from the beginning, was getting oppressive. Breathing took effort; even the seat back seemed to crowd, to crush from behind. Eedo imagined being caught in a garbage compactor. The image didn't do him good. He tried to make it go away, but it sank roots in his mind: telling him that close quarters were getting closer, closing in.

The sensation became unbearable. Eedo tried to say something, to alert Lars maybe, tell him to turn off the compactor, flip the switch—anything. *Anything* . . .

But words couldn't escape Eedo's mouth. Nothing could escape this pressure . . .

The car swung into a tight left turn. The boys in back tilted, rearranging their points of contact, easing somewhat Eedo's sense of confinement. He discovered he could breathe again.

Then he discovered that outside the car, the world was spinning. Left-to-right. Around and around and around . . .

No, the *car* was spinning—because it was still turning. Lars was driving in a circle. Industrial walls swept by, the headlights streaking across them, over a dirty sign that said ACME DRY CLEANING—the headlights seemed to rotate these objects around the car. The lights of the other car did the same: turning, turning, painting an encirclement of shabby facades. Eedo felt the pressure again. This turn just wouldn't stop. It was locking him into a new, equally horrible crunch.

Then abruptly the movement stopped. The boys in back lurched, took a different tilt. Again Eedo could breathe.

But he felt so dizzy. And the windshield was glowing much too brightly. The glass whited out, seemed to melt like something in a science-fiction flick . . .

The cars had stopped face-to-face, Eedo realized. Across a ten-foot divide they now vaporized each other with maximum high beams.

In the glare the heads of Ralph and Lars showed up as blots that somehow fizzed and crackled around the edges. Ralph's blot said slowly, menacingly, with all the warmth of an alien invader:

"Puppies, it's time to play."

From the roof of the derelict Acme Dry Cleaning plant— Through a pair of night vision goggles— Watching— Watching the young men pile out of

*the cars— Watching them spill into the fire of
headlights come eye-to-eye— Watching them
stumble giddily, dreamily, through the fire—*

*The face behind the goggles catches a
gleam— A faint gleam, thrown from a window
slamming shut in its door— Faint, but enough to
cast shadow into the pockmarks— Into the pits—
Enough to illumine, just for an instant, the
unearthly gray-yellow pallor—*

Eedo didn't feel on solid ground. The fusion of
the cars' headlights threw quite a glow,
enough to see by, but what Eedo saw kept
shifting. The pavement was shifting—it felt
treacherous, sandy in places, gooey in others.
The ACME DRY CLEANING sign looked insub-
stantial, even carbonated, as if it were composed of tiny teeming bubbles. The air itself
was shifting. Mutating. Eedo realized something that awed him. The air held numerous
mutating substances that he'd never noticed
before—but now could see, taste, *commingle
with* . . . for the first time . . .

"Eedo!" someone called, the voice rip-
pling the air, leaving slipstreams of substance
that pulsed here, writhed there. Ancient patterns here—a Chechan carpet, rearranging its
nuances mid-air. Shifting. Going deeper . . .
gorgeously deeper. But over there . . . Eedo

blinked. He shook his head, stared at the furnace of light between the cars.

His buddies splashed through it like kids at play. Yelling. Laughing at everything, at nothing. They were calling him over. "Eedo, come! Come in the fire . . ."

The fire, thought Eedo. *Gehenna's purifying fire* . . . The fire that awaited the weak, the infirm. That would incinerate this corrupt, stupid world . . . he staggered toward it, entered it, arms outstretched for balance. Ice-white heat—shifting swarms of light—it felt cold, the fire. Not burning—Eedo moved through unscathed. He took heart from this. He felt deep relief, for the coldness seemed a sign. It told him that like his companions, he was strong. Worthy. A man of faith and discipline . . .

But wait. His companions . . . Eedo gaped. They were howling. Barking. Baying like hounds . . . the dog game, he thought with a shiver of panic. His panic soured. It mutated into something different, something like terror . . .

The guys' heads were taking nonhuman shapes. Eedo watched them become the heads of dogs. Hellish dogs, howling hellish dogs—their jaws snapped. The fangs gleamed . . .

They'll eat me, Eedo thought. *Devour me*

whole—one of the dog heads lunged near. Eedo smelled its rank breath, felt a scalding spray of spittle, and then suddenly it wasn't a hound coming in for the kill. It was just one of the guys. Dylan. His buddy Dylan, putting a human mouth to his ear. Whispering, "Hey, man—*run*. Get away while you can."

Eedo saw truth in Dylan's eyes, the urgent truth of a warning. He whispered, "What?"

Dylan didn't reply. He walked away. The others walked away too, out of the lights—human now, a sense of finality in their movements. Eedo watched Ralph drain a Corona, toss it at the dark entry to the ruined dry cleaning building, and get in the car. Then the others were getting in the cars. Time to leave, Eedo thought. I'm going with them . . .

However, they were slamming doors.

"Wait," Eedo said shakily.

They looked at him through the windows, their eyes stony, knowing. The cars' engines ignited. Then the stereos ignited, sending a throb of bass lines into the night.

"Hey!" Eedo exclaimed.

Both cars backed up with a squeal of tires. Eedo stood transfixed in lengthening headlight beams, in a welter of bass lines echoing off the dark buildings. The cars stopped, giving him faint hope.

But then one sprang forward, directly toward him. At the last instant it veered, missed Eedo by inches. He broke into a dank, metallic sweat. Now the other car was coming—it also missed, just barely, leaving Eedo weak on his feet, paralyzed with fright. The cars started circling in tandem, like wolves coordinating the torment, the guys leaning out the windows yelling at him, jeering him. Eedo quaked; his mind slid, drained, lost its wits. Headlights, taillights trailed luminous blurs, spinning a vortex that he knew meant death—he had to take Dylan's advice. He had to run.

So he did. In a direction not of his choice, the harrying cars made sure of that. They herded him toward the entry to Acme Dry Cleaning. Eedo darted through, sought refuge in shadow. His heart pounded. He whimpered, tried to keep a grip on sanity. Behind him the demon cars screamed louder—they were storming the place, Eedo was sure, seeking the shadow in which he hid. He bolted from it and ran deeper within.

On a catwalk near the high ceiling— Through the night vision goggles— Watching the terrified

*boy flee the cars— Watching him make his way
by moonlight that seeps through glass bricks, shattered windows— Watching him stumble toward
his destiny— To the place where rustwater sprin-
kles the floor—*

Onward Eedo flailed, bumping into things, slipping on grime, junk. A faint light glowed further in. Eedo headed to it. He felt safer now,
just a little. The cars' music was fading . . . He
rounded a corner into a huge empty space.

Thirty feet overhead a bare bulb dangled,
for some reason lit. Glitter sparkled on the
floor beyond. Cautiously, Eedo approached
the glitter. He found a puddle of discolored
water in which lay shards of glass, fragments
of mirror. A steady sprinkle pattered into it.
Eedo looked up to find the source. The sprinkle descended from a broken pipe. Something
plopped on his shirt. A stray droplet. Rust-
colored, Eedo saw with a start.

A sound echoed in the dark above. The pat-
tering sprinkle muffled it. But Eedo was certain
he'd heard something. A soft flapping noise.

Bats? He stared upward and shuddered.
Something gliding there? Hovering?

*Flying— Aloft now, no need for night vision
goggles— On wings now, a different form of*

vision in play— Watching the boy below— He stands near the pool of a thousand glitters— Face upturned, pale, afraid— Helpless, weak— Very afraid—

Something flitted up there, Eedo was certain now. Something big. Eedo glimpsed wings. No, *they're much too big* . . . But yes, wings. Batlike membranes, dipping through the dark. A head poised in between. A head with a snout, a hound's head. Eedo saw a glimmer of jaundiced eyes . . .

Suddenly the creature dove at him with taloned claws outstretched. Eyes gleaming, the snout baring fangs . . .

Eedo let loose a strangled scream.

Closer— The boy by the glittering pool comes closer, closer— His eyes widen and roll as he screams, he's gripped with fright keener than any he's ever known—

Eedo crashed into the puddle as the creature hit, his arms flailing to fend off the talons, the monstrous houndlike snout. To no avail, for the jaws possessed infernal power, as did the talons—a great claw pressed into his chest, driving breath from it. The brilliant yellow eyes glared without pity—portals to damnation, to a damned soul. The snout curled, shivered, and bared fangs; with one stroke it shredded Eedo's upper lip. He shrieked, spattering the snout with blood. It continued to savage him—Eedo writhed, his screams penetrating every corner of the complex.

But there was nothing he could do. Except meet his fate on a bed of glinting glass, in a rusty puddle now getting rustier, face-to-face with the beast.

The gleaming eyes came closer. Eedo stopped breathing as they inspected his head, what was left of his mouth. Talons forced his jaws open; pincerlike, like a thumb working in concert with a finger, two of them reached inside. *No*, Eedo thought, sure the beast would rip out his brain, snatch it through his mouth's soft roof. Out ripped his tongue instead. A crimson flap—the creature swallowed it whole, sent the thing down its gullet with an effortless gulp. Eedo gargled blood. His throat welled with hot copper, hot salt, and he entered a new zone of fright.

A zone of searing concentration. A place where lucidity and horror merge: where lucidity and horror become the same thing. Again the two talons reached in his mouth. Their tips probed the carnage there with precision, as if looking for something, and they found it. A molar. They gripped the tooth with extraordinary power; then yanked it out and tossed it in the puddle.

Back they came for another tooth. Then another.

As the talons used his mouth as a kind of entertainment lounge, one steadily more bloody and plush, Eedo realized something that sent him deeper into the zone of fright. The beast was taking its time. Its methodical, surgical time. No rush. No need to wrap things up quickly.

Eedo would die with excruciating slowness.

Faith, he thought. Discipline. I've lost them . . . now I'm paying the price.

The beast continued its relentless plucking.

From the darkness above, sprinkle pattered into reddening water.

MILLENNIUM
CHAPTER

2

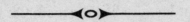

Summer sun filled the garden of the yellow Craftsman-style bungalow. Frank Black descended the porch steps carrying pliers and two large light bulbs. He walked across neatly trimmed grass to a ladder propped against the bungalow's side. Up it he climbed, to the motion-detector security fixture he'd installed on the roof's fascia board.

It was a good day for this kind of work. Warm, airy, fresh. Fluff-ball clouds dotted the sky, cotton-white against the blue—no threat, not yet at least. Nice weather. Especially for Seattle, city of mist, fog, lashing storms.

"Hey there!" called a voice from below. Startled, Frank turned. Jack Meredith, the next door neighbor, stood on the lawn, his broad face beaming. "Saw you working up there," he informed Frank. "Putting in a security light, huh?"

Frank smiled faintly. Jack Meredith's early retirement hadn't idled the man. On the contrary, it had given Jack a new career as full-time busybody. "Yeah," Frank said, his voice soft but penetrating. He started screwing in one of the big bulbs. "Days are going to start getting shorter," he continued. "Lights will be nice for Catherine if she comes home from work late."

"Oh," Jack said with interest. "Your wife get her job?"

"Yeah," said Frank, putting in the second bulb.

"Terrific!" Jack exclaimed. "What's the name of what she does again?"

"She's a clinical social worker," Frank said patiently, using the pliers to adjust the mounts. He liked to finish a job well, get it right down to the last detail. The angle of the lamps he changed slightly. That about did it. A little wiring work was all he had left.

"Oh, right," Jack was saying. "Yeah, sure—clinical social work. Hey, Frank. You got all the tools you need?"

Frank cast him an amiable glance. "Jack," he said, "I think I'm squared away."

The front door swung open. Two bundles of energy sped out—Jordan, Frank's six-year-old daughter, and Benny, Jordan's puppy. Catherine followed more sedately, her face pleasantly oval, smooth, and bright-eyed amid her wavy brown hair. Frank smiled at her. In his austere, weather-honed face, grooves deepened.

"Frank?" she said.

"Yeah?" he replied.

"You've got a phone call," Catherine told him. She said it casually. In a way indicating to Frank that the call could be important.

"Daddy!" Jordan yelled as Frank climbed down the ladder. "Did you make it work yet?"

"Almost, honey," Frank said. He stepped onto the grass and stooped to pick up his girl. "What have *you* been doing?"

"Playing with Benny," Jordan said happily, her face radiant in the sunshine. "Teaching him tricks!"

"Tricks?" Frank inquired as he carried her back up onto the porch. Benny followed, snuffling excitedly. "What kind of tricks?"

"Secret tricks," Jordan replied with grave conviction.

"I see," said Frank. "Well, you better not tell me about them, then. If they're secret." He winked at Catherine, handed her their child, and entered the house.

Catherine gazed at the avidly watching Jack Meredith. "Hi," she said with a sweet but somewhat perplexed smile.

Jack grinned, pleased that Frank's absence wouldn't put an end to neighborly discourse. "Hi," he said brightly.

The phone lay on the buffet counter that divided the hall from the kitchen. Frank picked it up and said, "Hello?"

A familiar male voice replied through the earpiece, "Hello, Frank? It's Peter Watts."

Frank's grip on the phone tightened. Watts was a member of the Millennium Group, the organization for which Frank did occasional investigative work. "Yes, Peter," he said.

Watts said, "I'm down in San Francisco. I've got what could be a multiple homicide here, possibly something a little more involved."

Something a little more involved. Frank took a deep breath. Behind him, Catherine and Jordan were entering the house. He didn't want to say anything or do anything that might give them cause for alarm. At the same time, he knew that the "something" Watts mentioned had to be grounds for serious alarm. To Watts he said quietly, "Do you want to send me the details?"

"I could do that, Frank," Watts replied. "But the *lack* of detail has created a high level of concern. I really think we could use you here."

Frank watched Catherine fill Ben's water bowl at the kitchen sink. No question about it now. Watts was on to something. Something that Frank, despite the tang of dread in his gut, knew he had to deal with. "Right," he said. "I'll make the arrangements."

He hung up. Catherine was watching him now. Frank gazed back, sustaining eye contact for several long moments, as if to tell his wife that things were okay. But of course, things weren't okay. Awareness of this transferred between them, a wordless understanding born of honesty, tenderness, and a great deal of harrowing experience.

Catherine didn't flinch. She had learned how to deal with these situations. "Was that someone from the group?" she asked.

Frank nodded. "They've got something for me to look at down in San Francisco."

"Soon?" Catherine said carefully.

Frank moved to the front door, paused there. "Yeah," he said. He turned, resumed contact with Catherine's luminous pale eyes. "Right after I finish up wiring that light."